NEPHLIM RETURN

TOTAL CHANGE

Also by Clifton H. Bush:

The Third Prophecy, 1994

The Incumbent, 1996

The Wheat From the Chaff, 2004

THE NEFILIM RETURN

TOTAL CHANGE

Clifton H. Bush

FABCO INC.
INDIANAPOLIS, INDIANA

The Nefilim Return is a work of fiction, however the underlying research is factual. Any resemblance to actual events, locales or persons is entirely coincidental.

Copyright © 2008 by Clifton H. Bush

Published by Fabco Inc.

ISBN 0-9643612-1-3

Cover and interior design by Book Works, Inc.

First edition — January 2008

I dedicate this book to Karen Jean, my wife of many years who, through her support and encouragement, this book has been written. I also dedicate it to the men and women of all ages who have sought truth and struggled mightily against the forces which rewrite history and warp information to promote their own agendas. To all of these, my greatest respect and admiration.

The Winged Disc emblem on the facing page is the symbol for the planet Nibiru, the 12th planet in our solar system. It has an ecliptic orbit that enters our neighborhood every 3600 years, passing between Mars and Jupiter among the particles of the asteroid belt. The clay tablets from Mesopotamia call this belt "The Hammered out Bracelet" or is referred to as "Heaven" in the Sumerian texts. The significance of this symbol is that it's found painted, carved, imbedded or otherwise displayed on virtually every surface imaginable in the cradle of early Human civilization. It's symbolic of the planet from which the Nefilim or Annunaki came to colonize Earth and eventually create the Black Headed People who are our direct ancestors. Look around! The Winged Disc emblem is everywhere even today. Look carefully at anything Egyptian. I even have an American made automobile which proudly sports a symbol that looks surprisingly like a Winged Disc. Now, let it lead you through a story that although written as fiction, contains a very factual basis.

—Clifton H. Bush

The Nefilim inhabit the planet Nibiru just as we Human beings inhabit the planet Earth. The word Annanauki is the name given to 300 high counsel members who are the leaders of the Nefilim.

—Bonnie Lange

CHAPTER
1

Don Neal was looking out the window of his fourth-floor condo office, struggling to find the right way to call a United States representative a creep, pervert and all-round crook without using those most descriptive words—exactly! Don was known for getting the message across just short of being liable for slander. The telephone ringing broke his concentration, for which he was less than happy at the moment. He answered in his usual brusque voice.

"Don Neal!"

"It's Chris, Don. Got a minute?"

"For you, I've got all the minutes you want. Good to hear from you Chris. What's up?"

"Something *considerably different*. I need to talk with you about it as soon as possible. Are you and Jeannie going to be in town for the next few days?"

"Well . . . yes! Are you coming in?"

Donald Patrick Neal, ex-marine, ex-war correspondent, ex-political writer and current columnist published in several hundred papers, quickly focused when he heard *"considerably different"* from his friend of many years. He and Chris McIver had grown up together. Theirs was the friendship that started in the third grade. They did Boy Scouts, discovered girls and cars, and grew into young manhood together. Where Don had dumped the military and warmongering for chasing the world of written words, Chris had stayed in the air force, rising to the rank of colonel. Outside of his column *That's the Way It Is*, Don was well known for his expertise in Biblical and religious history. Don's wife Jeannie was his primary editor, a fine writer on her own, and the prettiest and softest part of an old curmudgeon. He, along with Chris, was particularly interested in the clay tablets found in Mesopotamia over two hundred years ago and the story they told about the Nefilim and our relationship to them.

Chris had recently retired from the military as a full colonel. Because of his interest in religious history and ancient history in general, he had gained a respectful following in archaeological circles as a thorough and exacting researcher. He completed his PhD in anthropology and archaeology while doing some base relocation work for the Air Force, mainly in the middle east. This gave Chris some up close and personal experience with this region of earth that held so many secrets of Human origin.

Chris married Nancy Ryerson, a willowy beauty, formerly a special assistant in the pentagon and ex-air force as well. She and Chris shared the same passion for things hidden and arcane. Of course, Don had been the best man at the wedding and all four got along famously. Chris and Nancy still lived in suburban D.C. while Don and Jeannie lived in Indianapolis, Indiana. It had been about six months since Chris and Don had talked . . . which wasn't unusual!

"What do you mean, 'considerably different', Chris? With everything we've seen, 'considerably different' has to be pretty 'off the wall' special."

"It is! Do you remember an air force general named Edwin T. Berkowicz?"

"Of course! Project Blue Book, Area 51, UFOs and such. Didn't Nancy work for him at one time?"

"Bingo! He's resurfaced. He disappeared after resigning from what ever he was doing in the field of alien contact."

"You're kidding! I've never met the man."

"I had only seen him once! And that was at our wedding. He slipped in right before the ceremony and left immediately after. God, was he imposing."

"Imposing how?"

"He's a good 6'8" and well over three hundred pounds. His hands were like hamhocks and he looked right through me. I've seen big men, but never big like he was. He stood in a little anteroom beside the chapel . . . by himself, and just smiled when the minister said I could kiss the bride. When I looked his way again, he was gone, simply disappeared."

"I just felt a little 'medium chill' run down my spine, Christopher. What's Nancy saying?"

"She's elated! She had told me a lot about the man some time ago; he was a real father figure to her; really supported her and helped her out when she needed help. She had a really hard time when her first husband was killed in a training accident. I know she hasn't heard from him in years."

"What's he want, Chris?"

"I don't want to talk on the phone about this right now, Don. Only this! Nancy and I have met with Ed and we all want to come to Indianapolis pretty quickly to meet with you and Jeannie. What he has to say is right down your alley . . . and mine. It deals with things we've spent many hours over many years discussing. He wants to share some information with all of us . . . together."

"What the hell, Chris! You know me, let's get it on. But why me too?"

"He says he's read your columns, knows we are friends and knows your interests. You in?"

Don didn't answer immediately. Chris could almost hear Don thinking and didn't say anything more.

"Chris, we've had some pretty unusual experiences together. With General Berkowicz involved, you couldn't beat me off with a stick. You bet I'm in!"

"Good! We'll leave in the morning and get into the airport just before noon. We'll call you to pick us up. Ed has arranged a private plane for us and Nancy will do the flying. If I'm lucky, she'll let me co-pilot. She's better with the little ones than I am . . . and she knows it. I'll bet she could handle a B-2 just as well. Anyway, she's on the phone right now filing flight plans, so we're on our way."

* * *

It was out of the question that Chris and Nancy would stay anywhere but with them at their downtown condo. Jeannie spiffed up the extra bedroom, laid out the towels and extras that they had enjoyed during their last visit. Don made certain they had the right amount of mixings for the perfect martinis they all enjoyed. There was a little consternation about what Ed might want and where he would stay but Don was non-plussed, "We know the couch isn't long enough," and "I'll bet he'll drink whatever we do . . . and more!"

The call came during cereal and coffee. ETA, one hour. Don and Jeannie pulled out of their underground garage and headed west with a quick fifteen-minute trip to the airport. Chris and Nancy were waiting outside the private hangar, each with an overnight bag. Quick hugs and into the car, they quickly headed home.

"You're still driving the same old Buick?" Chris said softly from his seat beside Don."

"Until they build a better one and give it to me, yes. Suits me fine and you're not going to get my goat about it on this trip . . . either!"

"Seriously, Don, why do you keep the same car for so long . . . what is this one, twelve years or so?"

"That's about it! It has a great V-6, supercharged and now mid-sized by today's standards. Look at it! Beautiful leather, easy to handle and paid for." Don flashed a sinister smile at Chris, "And I have an ejection seat on the passenger side for smartasses who make fun of my good old car."

Nancy and Jeannie were in the back seat, catching up on what they were interested in, generally ignor-

ing the front seat for the moment. Don, in his inim-
itable way, got right to the point. Nancy and Jeanie
tuned in.

"Where does Ed, and it certainly seems odd calling him simply Ed, want to meet with us?" Don asked.

"He said he would be at your place for cocktails
around five."

"Does he know where . . . ?"

"I . . . we didn't question him. You can bet he knows
where he's going and he'll be there at five." Nancy
said softly.

Coming back into Indianapolis after an absence of
some time, Chris couldn't help but notice the increase
in traffic. The city looked as clean as ever with buildings reflecting the sun into a glittering kaleidoscope
of passing colors.

"This city looks different every time I get back.
Sure doesn't look like the same place when we were
kids." Chris mused.

"Nope! The old 'cornfield with lights' is gone and
they don't even roll the sidewalks up at dark like they
used to when we were kids. Downtown is a lively
place these days with all the sports activity and really
good restaurants. Magnificent hotels and the Circle
City Mall make all the difference.

"Anymore, Jeannie and I eat out most of the time.
You can find any kind of food imaginable within

walking distance from our condo. Trying to stock the fridge for two gets tougher and tougher all the time. Anyway, neither of us wants to clean up the kitchen after a chop-chop mix-and-mash session."

Don swung the car into a down ramp and swiped his entry card. "We've enjoyed this place and we haven't changed it much since your last visit. You get the same room with the dust recently rearranged."

Ordering sandwiches, getting luggage distributed and making small talk ate up the afternoon hours. They had agreed to wait for Ed and let him set the agenda for their meeting. This was hard to do, especially for the ever-eager, ever-inquisitive Don Patrick Neal. Jeannie and Nancy, however, had no difficulty in passing the time with each other. They had known each other for about ten years now and often e-mailed and called one another to keep in touch. Typically, Don and Chris weren't as diligent with their long-distance relationship, but seemed to pick up right where they had left off when opportunity presented itself.

*   *   *

Five o'clock was rapidly approaching and no one acted indifferent. In fact, the atmosphere was pretty intense. Don hovered by the intercom, waiting for the announcement of Ed's arrival. At five o'clock on the dot there was a knock on the door. Don looked at the intercom in a funny way and walked to the door and opened it. To this day Don will not admit his mouth dropped open when he saw Ed Berkowicz for the first time. But it did!

There stood a man as big as the doorway. His military-style crew cut was a dark gray; campaign and battle ribbons and medals set off the four stars on his shoulders. His craggy features were as chiseled as Mount Rushmore. His eyes were neither unkind nor hard but were piercingly blue and slightly squinted with weather lines accenting the appearance of intense observation. No one in the room moved or said a word.

Slowly, a huge hand was extended toward Don and a genuinely large smile spread across a very pleasant face. "Mr. Neal, I'm Ed Berkowicz . . . and I understand a man can get a decent martini in this place." Don managed to regain his composure, accepted the outstretched hand and motioned Ed into the room. Upon entering, his gaze went immediately to Nancy, and then to Chris, who stepped up and took Ed's hand in a firm shake.

"It's good to see you two again this soon . . . and thanks for setting up this meeting so quickly. Let's see, the only one I haven't met yet is this lovely lady . . . Jeannie Neal?"

Ed stepped toward Jeannie and offered his hand, which she delicately took.

"A pleasure to meet you, general," Came out of Jeannie's mouth. Her eyes were wide open as she looked up at this huge man.

"Your eyes are quite beautiful, Jeannie . . . and thank you; I am indeed a 'gentle giant'."

"Did I say that?" Jeannie said with a surprised look on her face.

"You certainly did, and thank you again!"

Don hadn't moved from inside the door, but stood watching Ed, somewhat awed by the size, grace and style of this four-star general. Ed turned toward Don and with a mischievous humor said, "And about that martini?" It was like someone flipped a switch and the animation began. Without a word, Don went across the room to the bar and everyone followed.

*　　*　　*

Don did the honors in record time. "Vodka, dirty, with olives all around?" They were soon settled around the rather large bar, which dominated the whole end of the family room. It was a curved mahogany beauty with lighted shelves, brass rail and appointments. The required mirror on the wall behind it was lighted from behind the shelves of exotic bottles. The glass itself was etched with the silhouette of the jovial barmaid on one side and the taciturn cowpoke on the other. The golden rim set it apart from the wall in striking contrast. The barstools were large and comfortable. Ed sat at the far end of the bar, Chris at the other end. The ladies were in between and Don was on duty, towel in hand.

When all were settled and martinis had been placed with the usual comments about large olives and great cocktail glasses, Chris took the floor.

"To our hosts and our special guest, cheers!"

All took a sip and Don was rewarded with the comments such as 'nectar of the gods,' and more.

"Don, the martini is great and your home is quite beautiful," Ed began,"and this bar, it's a work of art! Is everyone comfortable? Good!" Looking directly at Nancy, "Seeing Nancy again is like a breath of fresh air . . . she was and is quite special to me and a good part of what we will do here on planet Earth. Chris, your dedication to understanding the origin of your race, along with the help and contributions of your good wife, was the determining factor in my choice of you two to assist in our program of *exposure and disclosure*."

Don, you and Jeannie have labored long to bring truth and information to a public that is diverted from serious pursuits by so many trivial things. You have worked hard to get their attention—now we will help you get it. Thank you for welcoming me here to talk with you. You will be like family to me . . . and I like that very much."

"Where have you been for all these years, Ed?" Nancy asked.

"I have been on the 12th planet of our solar system, the planet Nibiru. When my work with Area 51 and Groom Lake was done to the satisfaction of my advisors, I was asked if I would like to be reunited with my birth mother on Nibiru and prepare for another very important mission on Earth. I immediately accepted. My military records were kept 'alive' and I was considered on special assignment. This lasted about ten of your Earth years.

"It was a marvelous experience to see my mother, really for the first time, to get to know her and many other Nefilim. The advances they . . . we have made in the past 2000 years were shown to me as an example of what would happen on Earth at the proper time. That proper time has come."

"Time for what, Ed?" Don asked with intensity.

Ed responded with the same intensity, "The time has come for knowledge that has been hidden to be brought to light and for those who have hidden it to be exposed for doing so. The self-appointed controllers of Earth matters are losing control for many reasons and they can no longer keep their 'domestic cattle' dumb. It's time for the Human race to be released from bondage and prepare to assume their unique place in the universe.

"My particular emphasis will be in America; however, this is a worldwide problem. It would seem that the wrong people are running the show all over the world and for the wrong reasons. In most developing nations, a very small percentage of the population has been able to seize control and intimidate the majority. In the third world countries, people are starving and being killed on a daily basis for mostly tribal issues. In countries where people are starving, food would be adequate if people were allowed to live off the land. Instead, they are herded and emasculated. There is too much interference by stronger nations on the weaker for control of labor and raw materials. In too many developing nations, the old ways and beliefs that have served these Humans for generations have been stripped away and not replaced by 'something of value' to them.

"Without direct interference, most of the so-called 'backward societies' would evolve into what they are capable of. Overzealous missionary efforts and enslavement of Humans by other Humans have always produced confusion. Interference is seldom good and Human evolution will remain uneven. All men are not created equal—certainly all by the same process, but some will always be . . . more equal!

"Let me offer the most relevant example. You know that about 430,000 years ago, the Nefilim were the first 'alien race' that came to planet Earth. Other inter-galactic races had noticed the planet but did not interfere. The Nefilim were few and the work they came to do required them to do heavy labor. It was finally decided to create a new form of life to do this labor for them. Their scientists combined a primate, indigenous to this planet, and the DNA of the Nefilim themselves. This produced the 'black-headed' people, the first Humans on the planet. They were bred as servant laborers for the Nefilim and were themselves alien to this planet.

"This dramatically changed the evolutionary process on Earth and transgressed against the accepted law of non-interference. At that time, and for selfish reasons, the Nefilim, infants in the universe them-selves, created a new species. The Nefilim have con-tinued to refine this creation over the millennia, but the fact remains, the Nefilim are responsible for this creation—and are now held accountable. More *refinements* are to come!"

"Held accountable?" Don interjected with raised brows, "and refinements?"

"Yes, and we hope we're not too late. Humans have progressed to the extent that they are a threat to vis-iting ships from other races, are probing outer space with sophisticated equipment and have the thermonuclear capacity to destroy every living creature and Earth itself. This is not acceptable.

"Therefore, my . . . our mission is to interrupt this destructive path. This is why I have come to ask your help, to join with thousands of others who are prepared to effect the changes necessary. You might say the Nefilim, with your help, are trying to finish what we started and help the peoples of Earth eventually join the other races of the universe who are very willing to help you on from there."

"That's quite a twist, Ed." Chris said, "We certainly need the help—but never in my wildest imagination did I think the Nefilim would be the cavalry to come charging over the hill. Matter of fact, the timing is sure right. Things are starting to look pretty hopeless . . . everywhere!"

"Are there more like you out there?" Don asked, "Are there more Nefilim here that are going to help?"

"Yes, Don, there are many all over the world."

"I knew it—*I knew it!* You couldn't, you wouldn't have all left and now you're here to fix some things that are broken."

"Right, Don. And the time is right for us all to come out and be known for what and who we are. I, like 'Gilgamesh' of old, am two-thirds Nefilim and proud to be chosen for this mission."

Ed straightened and moved his shoulders to loosen up. "Is anyone hungry? Dinner is on me and its dinner time. "I didn't come here expecting to eat in this evening," Ed said casually, "In fact, I will ask that you be my guests for dinner tonight and share a rather elaborate dining experience."

Ed stood and with a very slight bow said, "It may be a little unconventional and strange, but I would appreciate it if you would join me on the roof of this building in ten minutes. The doors are open and the weather is mild. I'll wait for you there."

With that, Ed turned and left the room, shutting the door behind him.

"I wondered how he got to that door in the first place," Don said. "The security in this building is extensive. You have to push a button, announce yourself, look at a camera and be 'buzzed' in. Now I know he didn't come in through the front door."

"Ed was always coming and going in strange ways," Nancy said.

"What does he have? A chopper on the roof?" Don said.

"No, it's not a plane of any kind. It's—different from that . . . I can visualize it and it's completely different," Nancy explained, "Listen now, things are going to get real unusual for all of us. We're going to see and experience some things only the hard-core Ufology/Sci-fi people could accept without batting an eye. We're going to bat our eyes a few times and be introduced to things not many have seen. This is a different Ed from the one I remember. He's softer and more open than I've ever seen him—and this I know for certain: we can follow him anywhere and have no fear. This man is our friend, and a more powerful friend one could not have."

Chris moved toward Nancy and put his arm around her waist. "Quite a comforting speech there little lady. I believe you-lead the way!"

CHAPTER
2

One couldn't miss the outline of Ed's large body silhouetted against the Indianapolis skyline as his framing reference. He stood at parade rest; hands locked behind his back, the body ramrod straight, his shoulders squared against the early evening light. When the door clicked shut and all four were on the roof, Ed turned and smiled in a very disarming way. He walked toward them.

"Thank you, Nancy for the kind words of reassurance." He glanced down slightly, "I'm not very good at those things. Thank you,"

Ed motioned toward a distant corner of the roof, "There is our conveyance!"

All four followed his gesture and squinted into the diminishing light to see what he was pointing at. The former Colonel McIver, B-2 pilot with several thousand hours in the air, saw it first. He just stood there, watching it take shape from its virtual stealth shield.

"My god! It's . . . a . . . " Chris almost stuttered.

"Not a flying saucer, Chris. It's simply a very efficient shuttle craft that gets us around quietly, quickly and almost invisibly." Ed explained in a matter-of-fact way. "Our chariot awaits to take us to dinner."

Don could make it out now. It appeared to be about thirty-five feet in length and was the size of a sleek houseboat without the windows. It was metallic silver without projections, antennas or anything that would keep it from looking like a big elongated cylinder. It sat directly on the roof without legs or anything that appeared to support it. It stood about eight feet tall, with nothing to distinguish the front from the back.

Ed walked over to the craft and stood at its center. With no unusual movement, an opening appeared, showing a pleasantly lighted interior with plush seating. Steps extended to the rooftop as Ed stood to one side and motioned for all to enter. Nancy and Jeannie entered first and found very comfortable seats next to each other. Don was next. He looked at the soft seating, the indirect lighting panels, and in particular the control panel. There was no steering mechanism, only ovals with different colored lights of varying intensity. The large captain's chair was turned to receive its master. Don sat down beside Jeannie with a little pat on her leg. Chris entered last, glanced at Ed and caught a look of guarded excitement.

"Quite an airship, general."

"Wait until you see the next one, Chris." Ed said with an impish smile.

*   *   *

There was no sound and no sense of movement when Ed sat at the control panel and passed his hand over a few pulsating lights. The screen in front of Ed, which could be seen by all, indicated that they were quickly leaving the city and heading upward. Just as quickly, the panel turned skyward in time to see the usual passing through clouds. The sun again became visible above the horizon.

Everyone was peering intensely at the lights when Ed said, "There it is, just a speck in the distance, and we're closing rapidly."

"What is it, Ed?" Chris asked.

"It's a mother ship. We will be at about 175,000 feet. It is quite large . . . about the size of the largest aircraft carrier and every bit as self-sufficient. It's virtually a city in the sky with capabilities earthlings have only dreamed about. Some of the Sci-fi representations come close because of information shared with a select few, but only close."

"Are there many of those?" Jeannie asked.

"Quite a few and they are positioned all over the earth at this time."

"Does the military know they are there?" Don asked tensely.

"Not really . . . not yet! We are constantly moving and are fully cloaked from satellite and radar detection, even the special detection used to locate and bring down what are called UFOs. We are quite certain that the various militaries would assume us to be a threat and take inappropriate action. Our threat is certainly not military—and I will fully explain that later."

The dot on the screen was approaching and rapidly filled the screen. A slight rocking was felt.

"We are entering the ship," Ed said calmly. "Dinner is close at hand."

The door on the shuttlecraft hissed open and Ed led the party out onto a moving walkway that entered an area of colored panels. Ed approached one of them and it opened noiselessly. They all entered and sat comfortably on a waiting minibus like conveyance.

When all were aboard, they moved immediately with a hissing sound that suggested pneumatic propulsion.

They rode in silence for a period that seemed like several minutes while soft music enhanced the mellow glow of indirect lighting. The conveyance stopped and the door opened to a corridor that sloped slightly downward toward an enormous open room that looked exactly like an elaborate dining room on a huge ocean liner. A beautiful young woman in a pale melon-colored uniform met Ed at the entrance, smiled pleasantly at the entire party and indicated that all should follow her. There were others in the dining room, but no one seemed to notice the new group.

The greeter stopped at an opening that appeared when she approached and indicated all were to enter. It was a smaller room, perhaps fifteen by twenty feet and graced on one side by panoramic windows from floor to ceiling that revealed a darkness punctuated by glittering stars. The centered table was set for dinner and two attendants began to hold chairs back for the ladies while all four unashamedly tried to observe their unusual surroundings.

Ed sat at the head of the table. Beautifully shaped glasses of wine and small crackers with a highly aromatic cheese appeared quickly. Ed was quiet with a slight smile on his face as, one by one, his four guests began to breathe naturally.

Don was the first to break the pregnant silence: "Just when you think you've seen it all, Ed Berkowicz stops by for a drink."

"I have no idea where we are or really how we got here, but this is the greatest rush I've had since . . . since whenever!" Jeannie let out.

Chris picked up his wine glass, examined it carefully, and said," Here's to a long lost friend of magnificent capabilities . . . who has brought us here for good reason—wherever it is and whatever we may be involved in, I'm glad we're on your side. Where are we and what's going on, Ed? You bet I'm impressed, but I don't think that's the objective."

"Direct and incisive as usual Dr. McIver. Where you are is in the bow of a great spacecraft from another planet that now proves it exists. They have been seen on Earth before and often but then generally underreported and quickly forgotten because they *cannot* exist. The most publicized time was in Italy in 1985 when a pope was murdered before he could expose damaging truths about the Vatican Bank and other secrets. Though thousands saw the ship, the press quickly dropped the story and it was hardly mentioned in other parts of the world, particularly in America, where UFOs don't exist.

"The objective is simple." Ed leaned forward and placed his hands on the table with fingers splayed. "

I must discuss with you the inevitable changes taking place on Earth. In spite of all the efforts to deny their existence, Humans will soon become very much aware of ships from outer space and the entities that bring them. There will be tangible and undeniable proof of what are called *alien life forms*.

"The movies of the western world have done much to both prepare you for this contact and mostly cause you to fear it. Very serious and dangerous people have intentionally done this.

"Let me assure you, there is no cause for the fear that has been planted by the disinformation machine. Movies like *War of the Worlds, Invaders from Mars* and such are meant to cause hate and fear. On the other hand, *ET, Close Encounters of the Third Kind* and the old classic, *The Day the Earth Stood Still,* tell the real story. Our neighbors from space have no agenda except meaningful and productive interaction . . . when possible. Now, in addition to the many capabilities we have given to the Human race, we passed on to you many things which proved that we, the Nefilim, needed greater understanding ourselves to prepare us for contact with other more advanced races of the Universe. The Nefilim have transformed themselves within the past 2000 of your Earth years. When we, as a race, left you at the end of the Age of the Ram, we left you to enter the Age of Pisces with many things that harm you today. Many of Earth's control-ling institutions have seriously retarded your growth.

"We also left with you many entities like me, prod-ucts of the Nefilim taking mates among Humans. This era is set forth in Genesis, chapter six of your Bible, particularly the New Revised Standard Version, where the Nefilim are again included in this history. It begins with *When people began to multiply on the face of the ground.* The vast majority of these Nefilim/Human entities were decent and productive leaders and workers. Some, however, harbored the worst of our traits: greed, pride, violent tendencies and lust for power. And then we gave you 'kingship.' Worst of all, some of our olden Earth-settlers taught you war for their own selfish and hateful purposes. Because of errant kings we appointed and our own flawed hybrids, you learned well . . . *and have not been without war since.*

"Today, war on planet Earth would mean the destruction of the planet and all life on it. We are per-ilously close to that disaster and the time has come to prevent it if at all possible. We think we know how to begin."

"Good Lord, Ed, I can't imagine how you can turn that all around." Nancy said in a soft voice.

"More easily than you think, my dear Nancy. Another thing we gave you was the need to *look up to someone* like in worship or believe in. This was a self-ish need on the Nefilim's part, intended to keep Humans from rebelling against their masters. This need that was hard-wired into the Human has been very successfully used by organized religion to oppress and control people. We built into the Human the strong requirement to reproduce. Even this primal urge has been abused to oppress and control through rules, stigmas and superstitions. Finally, the need for food, clothing and shelter has placed most in irrevocable debt to those who control the planet's wealth. Those who have the wealth want even more; therefore, they finance and perpetuate war, which is their greatest wealth builder.

"Now, the part I like most is talking about solutions. Love and hate are the strongest emotions of mankind—and they are so close together! Where love is creative, hate is destructive . . . mostly to the hater. We sense a gnawing need in most of Earth's population for less hate and more love, a true spiritual love that is inclusive and genuinely kind.

"Most people are coming to the conclusion that there is potential in love where hate is a downward, one-way street. People are awakening to the deceit of politics and politicians. People are seriously questioning the yoke of organized religion and 'God' for that matter and His part in their lives. People are tired of the incessant demands of attributing everything good to God but being told it's his mysterious way when things go wrong. A changing time in the affairs of Earth is boiling up. A rebellion against old orders, such as religions and governments that oppress, tax and control, is at hand. For all of this, the time is right."

"A complete and total change on the planet." Jeannie mused.

"Yes! Changing times, changing Humans and changing awareness that we are not alone in the universe and there is a new and better tomorrow. Total change!"

Ed leaned back in his chair and asked, "Anyone hungry?"

Like coming out of a trance, everyone kind of shook themselves and realized they were hungry. Like magic, food began to appear. The plates were warm with beef medallions and small slices of baby red potatoes. A small dish of greens with roasted pecans was served separately. It was delicious, and Ed explained he couldn't help but introduce a vegetable not found on earth to the meal. It was an immediate success. Rather quickly, the eating was ended and the table was cleared. More water, coffee and tea were served and it was time to resume. Ed waited until every one was settled and cleared his throat to signal a continuing of the subject.

"Do you recall from mythology how the great Greek tragedies were finally solved by 'Deus ex machina' coming down from Mount Olympus to sit above the whole mess and resolve the complex and convoluted ending?" Heads nodded in remembrance. "Well, you were right, Don. We are here to 'fix' some things and you're sitting in the 'machina.' In essence, that which the Human race has considered gods is arriving to help create the new tomorrow by resolving that which is convoluted and complex."

"God, what a concept! How in the world would you know where to start?" Chris asked.

"With a worldwide program of 'exposure and disclosure,'" Ed answered without hesitation. "Other extraterrestrial life forms, which are far more advanced and wiser, have charged the Nefilim and many entities like me with this task, which we gladly accept. It was the Nefilim who 'broke the rules' and interfered with the development of this planet. It will be the Nefilim and we who are products of the Nefilim who will do all within our power to 'fix' what we broke."

"Where do we fit in?" Don asked matter of factly.

"You and other Humans, with our assistance, will lead the way in exposure and disclosure. We will make it possible for you, and hold the doors open for you to walk through. We will protect you in the process . . . and you will need it. I was prepared for the United States of America, to understand its strengths and weaknesses, to know its processes and its people. This I have accomplished and have developed a plan that will begin the most far-reaching transformation since the great flood epic.

"I have chosen you to help execute the plan because of who and what you are. You four have proven yourselves to be spiritually and mentally capable of all required for acceptance of the next phases in Human development. You have the ability and desire and strength to bring about change. It will not be completed in your lifetime, but you will begin the process that will span many of your generations. "Yours will be the ultimate opportunity to *do something*." Ed looked at each one in turn and asked, "Will you go with me?"

Ed reached out and placed his right hand on the table in the center of the group. Nancy was the first to reach out and put her hand on top of Ed's; Chris quickly followed. Jeannie was next, her hand on top of Chris's. Don looked around at all present and slowly placed his hand on Jeannie's with, "No way old Don's not going on this one!" With that, Ed placed his other hand on top of all of theirs; not only dwarfing their hands with his, but also sending a tingling sensation through everyone that immediately bonded hearts and minds.

"So be it." Ed said sternly. "We are as one and we begin immediately." Ed released everyone's hands and again sat back in his chair. "We will return to your home now and I'll be back in five days to begin a process that will pave the way for necessary changes. I recommend that you go to family and loved ones in the next few days to assure them there will not be a great cataclysm or end-of-days event. We are not talking about *Armageddon* or end-of-days doom, but rather about a dawning of the new Earth, which will enrich us all with a wealth that cannot be stolen but only given away."

"What is this change? What's going to happen?" Jeannie asked.

"Please allow me to save the details for when I return in five days. Then, I will come to you and explain everything. But be aware, already earthlings sense a coming change, an uneasy feeling if you will, that the status quo is about to be shattered. Go about the next days carefully, be observant but speak little. Events will speak for themselves in the fullness of time. Come now, let's return to the beautiful planet Earth and prepare ourselves for a marvelous adventure."

CHAPTER
3

Ed did not accompany them back to the condo. He saw them off with a friendly smile and wave. Each looked at the other oddly when it was clear they had heard the same words from Ed, "I'll see you in five days, and then we will begin!"

"I remember now the many times I heard Ed speak to me from wherever he was—and wherever I was. It was a bond we shared," Nancy explained. "Now I remember so many things I am supposed to share with all of you . . . particularly you, Chris. You've been aware of my rather unusual 'sensitivity,' but it's not been a big deal. I have often suppressed this bless-ing/curse of mine, but now it's coming back and there must be a reason! It may be a part of what we're going to do with Ed."

Once again on the condo roof, the shuttlecraft seemed to just vanish. Don scanned the place where the shuttlecraft had been. Nothing! He quickly joined the others in the condo.

"Sure I'm going to lie down and go to sleep, sure I am. What about the rest of you?" Don said.

"No way," Jeannie said, "I may never sleep again."

Nancy went to the couch, flipped off her shoes and curled her feet up underneath a lap blanket. A slight smile crossed her pretty face; "I certainly don't feel like going to bed either . . . so much to think about."

The main conversation was about the airship and what they *hadn't* seen, the shuttlecraft and the meal. When it came to accepting that Ed was Nefilim, they didn't question it at all. Nancy had appeared deep in thought and began to talk in a soft, matter-of-fact way.

"Things were very rough for me back then. Tom, my husband of two years, had recently been killed in a training accident; I hadn't been able to shut out the voices that came from everywhere and I was so tired, just exhausted, depressed and overwhelmed with life. I usually flew on Saturday mornings, just to keep my hand in and get away from well-meaning but over-solicitous fellow workers and some 'newly appeared' interested males.

"I was at about 10,000 feet in a twin Cessna with unlimited visibility when one of the engines sputtered. I just looked out and realized I didn't give a damn. 'A quick way out' went through my mind. I made necessary corrections but actually said out loud, "I don't care, let them both quit." I started to spin and didn't seem to care, when a loud voice exploded in my head, 'NO! Start that engine and get back here. I'm waiting for you.' The voice was unmistakably Ed. The engine started and I brought it in.

"Ed was standing on the tarmac when I taxied in. He was supposed to be out of town, but he was there, waiting for me. I never went back into the pentagon. He met me for breakfast the next morning and took me to the Smithsonian, where I met Dr. Pagdu, one of the curators and my new employer. Those were two of the best years of my life, working with him in natural history and anthropology. And then, the best thing in my whole life happened, when one Dr. Christopher McIver, a tall, handsome man, walked in the door, into my life and swept me off my feet. That was over ten years ago and I didn't know until tonight that Ed Berkowicz had anything to do with it. I should have known!"

Chris chimed in, "I thought it was really strange when a four-star general came to the wedding and didn't stick around. I knew Nancy had worked at the pentagon for a very important officer but that in itself wasn't unusual. Nancy hadn't even seen him at the wedding. I can understand now why he didn't want to intrude on our special day. I soon forgot all about it. There were many more things to capture my attention—all were named Nancy."

"So that's where you learned about the clay tablets and the Nefilim, at the Smithsonian!" Don said knowingly to Nancy. "I've heard about Dr. Pagdu. East Indian and he lectures on Hinduism . . . a real knowledgeable guy and incidentally, a very fine person. He works at being Hindu, a way of life most westerners can't understand." Nancy added. "He never mentioned Chris to me except on the day he came into our office. The introduction even embarrassed Chris," Nancy said with a little giggle "You'd have thought Chris was the greatest archaeologist in the world and the foremost expert on the Sumerian clay tablets."

"Damned near is, gal." Don added. "With the exception of Zecharia Sitchen being the accepted pinnacle, Chris is close to the top. If you blow away the ones that are crippled by the paradigms of religion or indigenous tradition, he's the guy."

*   *   *

The smell of both bacon and coffee greeted Chris when Nancy gently nudged him. Soon, all four were at breakfast and plans were being made for the next five days. Nancy was going to fly back to Kansas and talk with her folks and Jeannie was going to try and talk to hers . . . again! Chris decided to stay in Indy while Nancy was gone. He wanted to see some of the old places with Don and pretty well stay away from persons he would love to talk with but would say too much to. He, like Don, didn't have living parents, just a few cousins he hadn't seen in years.

They decided on a good dinner out that evening and had one hell of a time finding a place that was quiet enough for conversation, had good food and service and would take reservations. They wound up at the Hyatt Regency Eagle's Nest.

Once seated, they each admitted to feeling a little strange, almost like they were strangers with a big secret and were trying to look and act normal . . . whatever that was! Everything had an edge to it. Everything looked and felt . . . *impermanent!* They ate a quiet meal and went back to the condo for drinks.

Don began to muse about his column when all were comfortable. He was the only one that seemed to want to talk, and the others were glad of it. Don started when he and Chris decided on going into the military. "Chris had always wanted to fly and I had always wanted to be a marine, like one of my cousins in World War II. This was the first time Chris and

I had been apart for any great length of time. The U.S. Marine Corps went well until it was time to get shot at. *That wasn't any fun at all.* When the tour was over, Don didn't reenlist. He was glad to be a civilian again. Chris said he liked the Air Force and intended to stay in. He was spending most all of his time in schools that prepared him to be an officer and live his dream of flying. We lost touch for a while." Chris simply nodded his head and continued to listen.

Don told of the early days, working in circulation at the paper, getting acquainted with the reporters and staff and finally trying his hand at writing in some contest. For a guy that flunked all English classes, this was an achievement and, he thought, an exercise in futility—but he worked at it and won! Pretty soon, he was writing more and more, and was starting to get paid for it. Then he was asked to write a story about war correspondents, and as a result, with the right support, he became one.

Two years of small and larger wars all over the planet had created a cynical, hard-boiled hater of war and those politicians and financial interests who fomented war. He finished his contract as a war correspondent, came home and met Jeannie. She worked for the paper and said she had watched Don grow and change from one bright-eyed wannabe to one damned good writer who could be great with a little help and encouragement. She was it!

"Jeannie made all the difference," Don continued. "We just put it together and made it work. I finally got the break I had been bucking for, a column of my own with an emphasis on politics. I got into it with gusto and pretty soon, a few other papers began to pick me up.

"And now, after I hit a peak of 264 papers, some of them are cutting back pretty severely. Mergers, sales, and belly-up tells the story for today's 4th estate. Most papers are in pretty deep trouble, as their subscribers go to the Internet for news." Don headed for the bar and wound up with one of his patented summaries. "Now, when you have about all the toys and things you want, when you've seen most of what there is to see and are looking for that next challenge, Major General Ed Berkowicz, the Nefilim, comes along.

"I have no idea what's in store for us or what part I . . . or we will be playing in whatever it is, but I'm ready! I'm ready for something that's wild and wonderful, beyond what I could ever imagine." Don walked up behind Jeannie and put his hand on her shoulder, "Are you ready too?"

*   *   *

They all went to the airport the next morning. Nancy had parked the plane in a private hangar, had it serviced, topped off with av-gas and checked out again. Chris had considered going but thought better of it. Nancy needed time alone with her parents. They were the salt-of-the-earth types that loved beyond comprehension and without reservation. Nancy was their only child. They were wheat farmers. You could hardly call them 'farmers' because their farm was in the thousands of acres, employed over 70 people, and everything was run by computers.

The Ryersons had built a special airstrip for Nancy, and greatly expanded it when she graduated to jets. Her Dad was a pilot, but he stuck to his high-winged, single-engine to oversee the land. He also flew for pleasure but stayed pretty close to home. He was on the local town council, had served one term in the state legislature and retired from politics quickly. "Those people don't say what they really mean and they know I know it. Damned uncomfortable and hardly workable." He would say. "Think I'll just raise wheat."

They all watched as Nancy taxied out to the concrete ribbon, waited her turn, quickly burned a hole in the sky—and was gone! The ride back to the condo was again strangely quiet. When they arrived, Jeannie said she had every intention of cleaning out her closet and generally straightening up and dusting. This is what Jeannie did when she wanted to think—or when she was disturbed. Not knowing which it was, Don and Chris began to make noises about 'going out' for a while. Jeannie encouraged them.

"Wanna go to the Rite for lunch?" Don asked.

"God, I haven't been there for years. About the same?"

"Food isn't cheap, but it's good and open to the public. It's about the third caterer we've had in there and they're doing a good job. I go as often as I can."

It was always a treat for Don to enter the Scottish Rite Cathedral on North Meridian St. As usual, he parked in the west lot and appreciated the covered entrance that had appeared in the last few years. Gone were the days when the Tyler sat at the doorway and greeted many he knew by name. These were the days of armed guards and cameras that saw everything. Chris also marveled again at the ornate appointments and beautiful wood throughout the Cathedral. They enjoyed a great soup-and-sandwich lunch.

"Remember the knights' room upstairs?" Don asked.

"Of course. My favorite room. We've had many a conversation up there—it may be time again."

"Let's go." Chris responded.

In days past, they might have opted for the stairs, but not now. The legs and knees just weren't as good as they used to be. They pushed the button and the elevator arrived. This is no ordinary elevator. The beautifully finished wood complemented an ornate cubicle that whisked them efficiently to the third floor. They walked around the wide balcony walkway that overlooked the ballroom. The crystal and German silver chandelier was lighted and cast its spectacular glow on the highly polished dance floor below. This is the dance floor that is actually built over springs, so that one could dance all night in unrivaled comfort.

This unique room was furnished for contemplation and conversation. Chris again walked from one side of the room to the other to see the eyes of the knights follow him. Many times he had noticed the appointments and symbolism of each knight, one Christian and the other Muslim. On first glance they were alike, but observation revealed how one held a sword and the other a staff, with differences in the armor. The eyes of both were especially expressive. The knights were fashioned from stained glass of incomparable beauty and were close to full-sized. You would notice something different every time you observed them closely. The light from the knights' window was usually all that was required to set a mood for contemplation. They sat in the corner of the room, not to be in the way in case others came to enjoy it.

"Do you have your mind around the Nefilim thing yet?" Don asked.

"I think I do, but it still feels like Hollywood or Sci-Fi. Never in my life did I think a thing like this would happen. What the hell is Ed going to do? Come down like a god from wherever and wipe out all the bad guys? What could anyone, even a Nefilim, do to straighten out the mess we're in? Is he going to talk to all the nasty people . . . the people who want to kill us and blow us to hell? Is he going to get rid of the poisonous partisan politics that have robbed us of our Republic? Is he going to dismember the Money Cabal that controls the wealth of the world? Is he by himself? Where else is something going to happen? Damn, Don! All I have is questions. How about you?"

"Same! What strikes me is that it's Ed . . . two-thirds Nefilim who is making the contact. Are the full Nefilim still 'too lofty' to talk with us Humans? Maybe they are for right now . . . but I'm going to ask."

"Ya know, Don, when you said you 'knew they did-n't all leave' it brought back many conversations we've had. How many Eds are there? How many people are there who are considerably less than two-thirds but nonetheless have many Nefilim capabilities? It's just like the children of Jesus and Mary and the countless people who are related 'by blood' to their progeny. How many other unions of Human and Nefilim, before and after the flood, produced a different breed of Human? God knows Humans have differentiated considerably in all respects but DNA proves we are all one race—and we were created in the image of the Nefilim. But what do the Nefilim look like? All we have are the Sumerian drawings."

"All we have are questions, ole buddy—and I'm not sure I'm satisfied with why we were chosen. What clout or power do we have? Yeah, questions."

"Ed said we would need some protection," Chris mused, "Are we going to be a threat—or represent a threat—and to whom? I'm interested in what we are supposed to tell those we care about—what's Nancy going to tell her parents? Get ready for a change? Sure! The Nefilim? Sure.

"Donald P., I think we're stuck until Ed gets back from wherever he was going. Four more days! That'll go pretty quick."

Don pulled out his cell phone and called Jeannie. "Can you think of any good reason why we shouldn't have fried chicken for dinner tonight?" A few seconds of listening assured him that was just 'hunky dory.' "Sure, we'll pick some up from the Club and be back about five, okay?" Don turned to Chris, "The club has the best fried chicken in the whole world."

Don headed north on Illinois Street and turned left on 30th. That took them by their old grade school, P.S. #41. Not only had it been renovated years ago to be a home for the elderly and infirm, but it was now surrounded by houses where the playground had been. Don slowed up a little for Chris to get a good look, but there wasn't much to see of the old school. Don took a few turns and they were almost in front of Chris's old house.

"They've redone that place several times in the past years," Don exclaimed. "Memories, huh?" They went out to Broad Ripple and past what used to be Broad Ripple High School Again, there wasn't much of the old school left. It was now huge by comparison and not much to bring back memories. "You can never go back, can you? I wonder if in four days, everything is going to be that way."

The White River Yacht Club had changed quite a bit in the past years, but some things never change. The bartender recognized Don immediately and held up the Scotch bottle. Don held up two fingers and blew her a kiss. They sat at a table for four next to the windows on the river side of the room.

"Come here often?" Chris asked. "The place sure looks good!"

"Yep, we sure do. Our best-kept secret in Indianapolis is now 500 members and a waiting list.

Things sure have changed. We're here pretty often . . . sometimes a couple of times a week in the off-season. There's a bunch of parties, birthdays and special events all year. When the boat's in the water, we're here most of the summer. We have a convenient dock, love the river and it's really our playground. We've been fortunate to find many good friends and acquaintances here. The place is affordable and my old Buick just naturally heads this way when the sun shines or it's time for a break."

"You wonder what kind of changes will come to a place like this." Chris said softly.

Don just looked out the window at the river he had loved most of his adult life. "I can imagine we will feel some of the effects of whatever happens. This place is really a microcosm of a small city. All of us are different—and probably will be affected differently. Yes! I imagine we will be affected too," he said slowly.

*   *   *

Jeannie opened the door looking radiant. Candles graced the table with soft music in the background. "What happened?" Don asked in genuine concern.

"I'm ready, is what happened. I've got my clothes straightened out, the dust rearranged and my favorite men in the house. Life is good! Nancy called in a little while ago. She's at her parents' home, feeling great and ready for a super visit. Now I don't want to spoil the mood," Jeannie continued, "but I called my parents in Muncie and they said they would welcome a visit tomorrow . . . you included, Don."

Don didn't say anything immediately. He just looked at his wife of many years with raised eyebrows, obviously trying to process a bunch of feelings and thoughts.

"Why now, all of a sudden, are they even admitting to my existence?" Don questioned. "Did you tell them the world was coming to an end or something?"

"Hardly!" Jeannie dismissed the thought. "I simply said that we're not getting any younger and it's time we set aside differences and act like family. Mom just said, 'that sounds like a good idea' and Dad came on the phone and told me how much he looked forward to the visit. Beats me, Donnie boy, but that's the way it is!"

"Wow! Chris said, "Sounds like a huge breakthrough to me. I'll take off for D.C. and get some stuff from our place for us and be back in plenty of time for day five."

*   *   *

Sam Middleton, Jeannie's father, swung the door open to invite Jeannie and Don inside. He was a small man, thin with wispy gray hair. He smiled and looked down when Don entered and softly muttered words of welcome. Jeannie's mother waited inside, standing in the center of the small living room with hands clasped in front of her. She was toiling with an apprehensive smile, and looked damned uncomfortable. Sam motioned to the couch for Don to have a seat and Jeannie quickly joined him. Don felt grateful there were no gratuitous hugs or otherwise false overtures Humans deceive themselves with. Sam went to his obviously favorite chair and sat down; Carrie Middleton stood beside him, a stout woman with a simple flowered dress tied at the waist. Her gray hair was tied back in a severe bun. She wore no jewelry. Her eyes were a pale blue and squinted as if she was having a hard time seeing.

"It's a couple of years since I've been in the house." Jeannie said nervously.

"Yes, it's been a long time. Now, we're a-sellin' it and going to 'assisted living.' Sam can't keep up with the work around here any more and believe it or not, this little place is too big for us now." Carrie shifted her stance a little. "We were a thinking you might want to see it one more time before it's gone!"

"You know mom, what I would really like to see is my old room. When I was a little girl, it was my castle, my dream world and a place to be by myself. I'd love to see it."

Without another word, Carrie turned and headed down the hallway to the first door on the left, opened it and motioned Jeannie in. Jeannie's eyes were big as she approached the door. She apprehensively entered and her Mom followed.

Sam leaned forward in his chair and looked at Don with a strange and quizzical look. You're an important man, aren't you, Mr. Neal?"

"Not really, Mr. Middleton . . . "

"Sam!"

"Thank you . . . Sam! No, I'm not important, but what I am constantly is a good husband to your daughter, whom I love very much."

"How long now?"

"We're coming up on twenty-six years."

"That long! I had no idea it had been that long." Sam looked pensively at the ceiling, then directly at Don. "We're different, you and me."

"We're both Human, Sam. That's a good place to start being alike."

"But we're God-fearing Humans. Are you?"

"I don't fear God, Sam. I don't live my life around what is said of God, but I have no condemnation of those who do. We each have to walk in our own light."

Sam started to reply but was startled to see Jeannie appear from the door to her old room carrying a big doll close to her chest, tears showing in her eyes.

"They haven't changed a thing in there Don. It's like the day I left it!"

Carrie Middleton was close behind Jeannie with the same stern look on her face. Jeannie went and sat beside Don, still holding the doll close to her. Sam wasn't finished with his and Don's conversation.

"I've read some things you've written about the 'evangelicals' and the power of the Christian Right. You don't seem to approve very much!"

"Sam . . . and Mrs. Middleton, I came here today to bring my wife to see her parents . . . who, for whatever reasons, have pretty well written her off for years. I haven't come here to debate religion or politics. I'm here so I can tell you what a fine woman and a good wife your Jeannie is."

Don was speaking softly but with undeniable authority in his voice. He could sense a hardening or stiffening of mind in both the Middleton's. He made an instant decision, stood up and offered his hand to Sam, who reluctantly took it.

"For whatever time it takes for you and Jeannie, I'll wait in the car. I have a good book to keep me occupied. I'm quite certain my presence here will not contribute to anything good for you and your daughter." Looking down at Jeannie, who showed not the slightest confusion, Don said "I'll wait for you in the car, honey. Take your time." With that, he left the house immediately.

Don had barely settled in with his book when Jeannie came out the door, pulling it shut behind her. She still had the doll. Firmly belted into the good old Buick, they headed south on old 37 in silence, no tears, no comments, just a feeling of emptiness and failure to connect. Finally, Jeannie broke the silence.

"They wanted me to pray with them . . . they actually wanted me to get on my knees and ask forgiveness for living in sin . . . with you, and everything else they consider unChristian." Don didn't say a word, but kept his eyes on the road and waited for more.

"I kinda took my cue from you, asked if I might keep the doll, shook hands with my father—*and shook hands with my mother*, for god's sake! I thanked them for seeing us and wished them success and happiness in their new living adventure—and left. They didn't say a word; they just kind of stared at me . . . almost like they were afraid of me! I'm glad to be out of there Don. It was like a foreign world."

"It is, Jeannie. More and more, it's a 'them and us' thing, all over America. In spite of everything we've learned over the last three hundred years or so, millions of people still pray to a six-foot, light-haired, Arian-looking Jesus that will take them to Heaven if they follow certain rules. People all over the world think we're nuts and over the top on Christianity, but don't want to really piss us off. I've seen more Christian fearing than God fearing."

*   *   *

Meanwhile, Nancy had advised her father by radio she was making her descent toward the landing strip and would circle the field once before landing. She gracefully banked the plane barely above stall speed around the strip, looking to see everyone piling into the big Silverado to come meet her. The touchdown was smooth as usual and she had barely finished the shutdown procedure before her Mom, Dad and the two oldest hands, were all waiting for the door to swing down. The hugs, kisses and pats were what love is made of.

There was nothing else to do but drive around the newest additions and improvements to the farm's buildings and equipment. People waved from everywhere work was going on and the big 'Welcome home Nancy' banner stretched across the driveway to the house. The house hadn't changed much over the years. It was a four-bedroom ranch with proper and necessary amenities but was in no way ostentatious or overblown. It was a home, not a showplace.

Traveling with basically the clothes on her back, Nancy opted for a quick shower and to change into clothes already laid out. Jeans and a plaid shirt were the order of the day. Hot tea was waiting when she walked into the family room, shaking drying hair.

"Nancy, you get more beautiful every time you come home," her father said with a huge grin. "And where did you get that plane? It's beautiful . . . and expensive! Hit it rich?"

"You remember Major General Edwin T. Berkowicz? He's come back into our lives in a big way— which I'll have to explain at a quieter time. It's his airplane or at least he has general use of it. All the codes and passes are in his name, which makes the airways pretty slick. Talk about clearance!"

Nancy's home coming was a big deal. Several neighbors came by, along with Nancys' flight instructor of years ago. He spent a long time with the airplane, asking questions about it Nancy couldn't answer. "I just know how to fly it, Jack, not build it!" Company and laughter continued into the late afternoon. Most of the neighbors had big farms and hands to feed and some evening chores to tend to. It was after the dinner cleanup up when Nancy and her parents were able to get some time alone.

"Able to stay long?"

"I'm due back in Indianapolis in three days. We're staying with Don and Jeannie Neal for a few days. Ed Berkowicz is meeting us there also. He'll probably want his plane back."

"What else will he want?"

"You're perceptive as usual, Dad. He wants the four of us to work with him on something terribly big— and that's why I'm here, to tell you what I can and tell you and Mom to expect something to happen that will change the way things work on Earth."

Nancy proceeded to tell her parents the whole story from the time Ed contacted her just a few days ago. Both parents listened with more than usual interest while Nancy gave them every detail she could remember up to this visit. They said not a word and didn't ask any questions. When she was finished with "And that's all I know to this minute," her father relit his pipe and her mother went to get some more tea.

"So, Ed is Nefilim?"

"He says two-thirds Nefilim," Nancy replied.

"Like Gilgamesh, Nefilim mother and Human father!"

"Yes, dad. I recall that was what Gilgamesh was— one of the 'old men of renown' from the Bible."

"You too have Nefilim blood, Nancy." Suddenly the buzzing began in Nancy's ears as every fiber in her body went taut. "I am far from two-thirds, but I have known all my life that I'm . . . different, and that difference was passed on to you."

"You mean my being a sensitive is a Nefilim trait? That it wasn't some curse all my younger life until I could control it? You know how many times it hurt me and made people stay away from me . . . but you were always there, you understood me, and . . . Dad, you too?"

"Yes, all of my life too." He laid down his cold pipe and rubbed his hands a little before going on. "Your mother and I have known for a while now that a big change is coming. I . . . we could feel it. It's been a very subliminal thing but very present. I don't doubt that everyone who has come to grips with their heritage, rather than losing their minds or jumping off a building, has quietly accepted what and who they are. Now it would seem we are being invited to either participate or observe, or both!"

Nancy's mom had rejoined them and quietly waited to contribute. "You can't imagine what these years have been like, Nancy. We knew what you were going through many times but were hesitant to tell you that Nefilim inheritance was involved. But look at you now. Vibrant, beautiful and married to one Christopher McIver, a virtual giant in his field. You have done well, my dear Nancy. We're very proud of you."

Walt picked up on that statement and added, "There must be thousands of us, Nancy, those who have one or more of the 'extra genetic switches' turned on that give us some unusual abilities—unusual to those who are afraid of these things, frightening to those who can't handle anything 'different' or attribute the differences to religious taboos or things of the devil—whoever or whatever in the hell that is."

The days went quickly. Nancy rode on the huge machines of wheat farming, took her old flight instructor and her parents for a ride in the little jet and generally had a visit full of laughter and love. They all knew that the time for Nancy's return had come and spent quality time remembering and looking forward to the future.

"I doubt this change will let your mother and me alone," Walt said. "All of my life I've felt there was a higher calling for me and I've been allowed to prepare for it. Finding that you're part of it makes me warm all over, Nancy. I guess we had better get on with it, and I doubt it will be long before we see each other again."

With tears in her eyes and a deep joy in her heart, Nancy thundered into the crisp morning air for a quick return to her friends and her husband in Indianapolis. The thought kept repeating itself in her head *let the games begin*. With a smile on her lips and anticipation of a great adventure in her spirit, Nancy McIver slipped quickly and smoothly through the clouds toward the east.

CHAPTER
4

At exactly five o'clock on the fifth day, Ed walked through the door to the Neal condo. Don had left it ajar intentionally; his way of acknowledging the reality of Ed and this whole thing.

"My martini, Mr. Neal? Vodka up, with olives and dirty, one cube for the tinkle, if you please."

Ed set several small packages down beside the door and advanced toward the bar, nodding to the women and shaking hands with both Don and Chris. Ed was clothed in what had to be the classiest looking jump suit in the world. The small chatter of 'how did the visits go' and simple forms of greeting passed quickly. Don was the first, as usual, to get down to business.

"What's the agenda, Ed? We've even been concerned about how to dress for the occasion."

"I've taken care of that," Ed motioned to the packages he brought in and pointed to his own garment, "but this is an evening of getting better acquainted and answering questions. I don't expect any of you to do anything without knowing everything you want to know. Get comfortable and let's talk, because tomorrow morning we go to work."

"At what, Ed?" Chris asked.

"At making the entire world, beginning with the United States of America, aware that they 'are not alone' in this vast universe and introducing the population to a good dose of honesty . . . for a change, that will revolutionize how we look at each other, how we treat each other and chart the course toward a much greater understanding of who we are, how we got here and where we are going! Are those enough answers?"

"That'll sure do for a start." Don whistled out an exclamation.

Ed looked directly at Nancy, "I hear you Nancy . . . and you're right. It's getting stronger, isn't it?"

"What?" Don asked.

"Nancy's ability to communicate telepathically—which she's had all her life."

"She's sublimated it for years now," Chris, said, "It was never a problem with us but it sure upset some others."

"Let me do what Nancy asked of me, and I'll say more about that later—in fact, much more. Nancy thinks I should share with you some of my background."

There was a general murmur of agreement. Ed looked at everyone in the room and then began in a clear, mellow tone of voice that, as Don observed, could be mesmerizing.

"My exact date of birth I don't know but it was in the year 1901. I hope I don't look my age . . . but my life expectancy is over 300 earth years. Were I to have stayed on Nibiru, my life expectancy would be considerably greater. My father, a Human, was killed while trying to protect a young woman from being raped by a gang of thugs. My mother, soon after finding no legal justice, found the culprits and dispatched her own. Soon after that, she left Earth for Nibiru, where she still lives. It was decided, I learned later, to leave me on this planet to be prepared for what we will begin tomorrow. It has indeed been that long in coming.

"My childhood was spent with various Nefilim families, similar to Nancy's, where I was trained and educated as an American. Well-placed solicitors and agents saw to my interests and needs. My only disappointments were not being able to play sports and seriously date girls. My physical and mental attributes would have made me look . . . too different. I went directly from high school to West Point, where I was prepared for leadership and war. Obviously, they were successful.

"I actively commanded battle groups in both the Asian and European theaters during World War II, and then was by design appointed to the super secret investigation of alien activity and technology. There, I became acquainted with the vast and powerful cover-up activities of our legitimate government, then the insidious activities of the 'shadow government' that wants to control everything about what they learned. I'll tell you more about that later as we get into our project. From the early 1940s I walked through many crash sites of extraterrestrial spacecraft and eventually worked with Operation Blue Book. I spent time at Area 51 and although I didn't see one, I was aware of live aliens they called Greys that were being studied. Had they known me as I am, I also would have been treated as 'an alien' and studied . . . to death!

"I was later reassigned to the pentagon, where I met Nancy, with the objective of learning about the military-industrial complex. I encountered the paranoia of the military regarding UFOs. I observed how anything related to UFOs was top secret and held under close control by a cartel called in the beginning *'Majestic Twelve.'* I was then invited to Nibiru where I saw my mother, still a beautiful young woman, and began preparations for my return to Earth. That was a little over ten of your earth years ago.

"Now, we are prepared for a mission of 'exposure and disclosure . . . and liberation! Quite frankly, knowing you as I do, you will quite enjoy watching this unfold."

"How are you going to do this, Ed?" Jeannie asked, "It does sound like the 'Deus ex machina' from the Greek tragedies. We've seen the machine, but the message? How in the wor . . . ?"

"You've got it, Jeannie. We are going to show them the machine, just one, and proceed from there. Governments of the world are never going to reveal the contacts with aliens they've experienced for decades, unless they have no choice. We're going to remove that choice and let rational peoples of the world know what has been brutally kept from them, all in the name of 'our best interests.'

"Our best interests, bull sh . . . !" Chris blurted out.

"Dr. McIver, how very profound." Ed smiled a genuine smile of mirth, "More to the interests of the religions, the military and the Money Cabal. The tools of their deception have been fear, ridicule, intimidation and, when necessary, murder. Any method will be used to 'keep the lid on' and keep the populace in place—under control.

"America is a bit different," Ed continued. "In general, Americans have been hounded into increasing debt to acquire *things*, diverted from more serious pursuits by filling our many coliseums with athletic endeavors, and seduced by slick, sexy advertising into being the greatest consumer nation in the world. Our children are targeted by Madison Avenue to do more of the same, all in the name of growth and progress.

"Too many Americans have been 'evangelized' into believing God is their personal day-to-day micromanager. Everything is God's will, God's way. Early on when the cross replaced the sign of the fish for the age of Pieces, the worst was feared . . . and we got it. When 'faith and belief' replaced 'fact and reason', America weakened. But now, comes the Age of Aquarius! Light must shine in all the dark and slimy crevasses. Exposure and Disclosure is the way of tomorrow.

"So we begin with America, where we are free to work ourselves to the grave to support wars we don't need or want, to support politicians who are captives of the Money Cabal, and raise children who are both in control and out of control. America is unquestionably the leader of the world in many things and indeed the greatest superpower since Rome. America has accomplished much and is within herself, a generous, giving nation filled with well-meaning people who are generally honest and good-hearted. On the other hand, it takes a whole lot of raw material and money to operate this land of plenty, and raw power to maintain the supply lines.

"All too often, what the rest of the world sees are those who will sell their mother for a profit or spill blood for an 'edge'. The politics of America? 'A republic, if you can keep it!' Franklin said. Unfortunately, we have lost it to special interests, professional politicians and laws that too often favor the lawless. Tightly controlled money interests, the world banks and those who 'live in the silence,' again crown succeeding Caesars and decide the next pope."

Chris impatiently asked. "So how are we going to change all of this . . . besides the machine, which will scare the be-jesus out of most everybody, what in the world can be done to address all of these things we all know are wrong?. How are you going to change people?"

"Let's finish with the 'deus ex machina' first, okay?" Ed said with a grin.

"By all means," Don chimed in.

"I don't blame you for being a little cynical and impatient here, Chris. My job is to set the stage and begin the play. Part of that is the setup, which we have done, and now comes the fun part . . . at least I think it'll be fun."

All eyes were intent on Ed when he said 'fun'. So far, nobody had thought of any of this as being a little bit funny. Ed caught this immediately and responded.

"Let's take this a piece at a time. It'll be tomorrow afternoon when the ship you were on will come in over the Atlantic and head for New York."

"My god, Ed! The military will go bonkers . . . particularly after 9/11!" Don sputtered out.

Ed held up his hand in the *wait a minute* mode and continued. "This will be after I have met with the white house and Chris has appeared at the pentagon. He will have all the necessary papers and passes to access the various situation rooms. He will tell them what the object is that approaches. He will present a one-page, three-paragraph letter to all concerned that contains all that needs to be known at this time. Some there will wet their pants, some will bristle and posture, but there are those who will not be surprised. There will be confusion, of course!

"The letter will state this craft is not from this planet and comes in peace. The craft will approach slowly for all to see and pause offshore. It will also declare that all weapons that could be directed toward the ship have been neutralized and they are to 'stand down' any and all military actions against the ship. There will be some panic and fear but the electronic media will assure the public that we come in peace. The craft will then continue inland and all will be encouraged to document the event as the first open and peaceful intentional contact from outer-world entities."

"What about the white house?" Jeannie asked. "What will you do there?"

"This will be my pleasure." Ed answered. "I will be with the president, the vice president and the speaker of the house, all alone with me in the oval office. No press, no advisors, no cabinet members, just the four of us."

"My god, Ed," Chris incredulously questioned. "How in the world are you going to be able to pull all of this off . . . into the pentagon, the situation rooms, and those three together at one time in the same place? What do you have, a magic wand?"

"Pretty close! Come on, now you don't believe for one second that just thee and me were going to pull this thing off. Many people have been in place for a long time coming to this point . . . many people with extraordinary abilities and a burning desire to get this thing done."

"Nefilim?" Jeannie asked.

"Many are, but many more are extraordinary Humans with the same burning desire to clean this mess up and prepare for a better world—extraordinary Humans just like you four. Believe me, it'll work. Neighboring countries will have their own *opportunities* and will not interfere."

Nancy had been unusually quiet until now, taking everything in and saying little.

Suddenly she came to full attention. "I'm seeing it, Ed! I can see where you're going . . . it's both beautiful and . . . brutal!"

"And effective, my dear Nancy. Particularly you can see the value of the plan, but let me continue for the others.

"The president of the United States et al. will not interfere or allow interference. There will be no orders except to '*stand down.*' We expect the media to be stunned and the population will be also. There is no way to eliminate fear from the minds of the populace except through the media, which *will* call for calm. It will eventually come as the craft continues into New York and settles above the United Nations Building. There it will remain stationary, without sound or interference of normal functions. No *The Day the Earth Stood Still* effects will be necessary."

"I see the picture," Chris said, "It will be like the War of the Worlds broadcast back in '38, but there are no monsters or killing machines. I can see the population eventually calming down and just staring at this one-mile-long ship from another world. Boy, that is going to change things . . . *no, we are not alone* . . . and what happens next if they *didn't* come to destroy us?"

"The 'what happens next' factor is going to be a real wake-up call," Nancy inserted, "It will change the way things are done on planet Earth, in a big way and in a big hurry!"

"The entire building will be humming with activity because the entire general assembly will be in session. The media will be fully staffed and by this time, the streets will be full of people looking at the spectacle of the huge airship. Some pulsating lights will be visible," Ed began, "as totally undetectable electronic impulses engulf the entire building and electromagnetically affect everyone inside. A trait that was built into them by their Creators, the Nefilim, will be stimulated and augmented *to the extent each one is capable.* It's a natural part of all of us that has been condemned by religion, coveted by sages and feared by most because they were afraid they were losing their minds. Tell them, Nancy, what's going to happen?"

Serenity surrounded Nancy as she smiled slightly, "That 'gift' that has both plagued and helped me in my life will be visited on all in that building. Each, to their own degree of capability will become a telepath

. . . that is, they will not only be able to know what is in the mind of others but will be unable to prevent others from knowing what is in their mind. *Deception and deceit will be impossible."*

Don spoke up immediately. "When these people can't lie to each other . . . or themselves, when the cover of diplomatic deceit is blown away, that building could empty out pretty quickly."

"Well, Mr. Columnist and political commentator," Ed began, "is that where it should stop?"

"Hell no!" Chris jumped in, "Where to next, Ed?"

Ed just smiled and looked at Nancy.

"I can't imagine we could pass up the white house and the congress of the United States of America, now could we?" Nancy said softly. "That whole damned house of cards will fall without deceit and deception!"

"It's our anticipation that it will at least undergo far-reaching changes which will allow for openness and candor with the American people." Ed added, "When the confusion clears, there will be much better and stronger leadership in matters that government should address rather than the issues forced upon it by the special and vested interests."

"We will no longer have the 'best government that money can buy.'" Don added.

"Where else is this going on?" Chris asked.

"It's worldwide, Chris. Every leadership element in the world is going to experience the same thing, differing only in how their leadership is. Even the third-world countries with tribal warlords will feel this thrust of candor and truth . . . and some of them value honesty more highly than the 'more advanced' nations. Deceit there could mean death, very quickly."

"Okay, I get the picture," Don said. "I think I understand what Chris and I assume Nancy is going to do tomorrow . . . I think I understand what you are going to do tomorrow . . . what will Jeannie and I do?"

"What you do best, of course. Gather information and reduce it to the understandable written word for the populace."

"You think the newspapers are going to survive this? They've become the most unreliable source of news there is. Talk about spin and half truths!"

"You'll not be writing for the newspapers, Don. Do you think advertising will survive as it is? Of course not! But the Internet will! Daily, yes daily, Donald Patrick Neal's web page, *That's the Way It Is*, will be read by a population hungry for the truth. They've learned to trust and respect your views and opinions over the years. Now, columns won't be spiked for goring someone's sacred cow. You can tell it like it is with all the backing you need. You'll have enough to keep you busy."

Don slumped back in his chair, a contemplative expression on his face. "A journalist's dream come true, but how is everyone going to get paid for working if everything goes to hell in a handbasket?"

"It won't be that way, Don. Commerce and business will continue with little disruption. Some 'so-called' leaders will fall on their swords and die or disappear from the scene in disgrace . . . some will turn around, becoming part of the solution rather than part of the problem. There will be less disruption than rejoicing."

"A nightmare for those who cheat, lie and steal and a whole new way of life for those who don't," Jeannie added.

*   *   *

Ed picked up the packages he had brought to the condo with him and passed them out. Each unwrapped one to find a beautifully fashioned one-piece suit like Ed's, made with a type of microfiber. It was silky smooth to the touch yet had a consistency that felt very solid and sturdy.

"Virtually indestructible." Ed said. "I always wondered how the young ladies got those jeans to fit so well on various shapes! This stuff answered my question—but it's not made of denim. The creamy color with gold piping gives the suit a touch of class and the cut will form to the body, not tight-tight, but comfortable. They are made to look classic, elegant, and suitable for formal wear as well as casual formal. The suit makes its own rules on fashion—it will be warm when you need it and cool when required.

"They are virtually fireproof, will repel sharp objects and even high-caliber bullets. They also have the properties of the shuttle craft you were in . . . you can meld into the shadows and be virtually invisible when still. These are your uniforms; this is the clothing of the Nefilim. Various types of this clothing have confused people when they were sure they had seen something."

"Do we wear these tomorrow?" Chris asked.

"You and Nancy in the pentagon, certainly! For my visit with the president and his people, I'll wear my military uniform, with all the spit and polish I can muster. That is very impressive for the marine security guards and in the oval office setting."

"How impressive will two civilians in jump-suits look in the pentagon, Ed?" Chris asked in all seriousness.

"You underestimate yourself, Dr. McIver. You will stand out like a sore thumb intentionally, Sir. Your visit is already preceded by your reputation, as one of the foremost and knowledgeable experts in the field of 'where we come from' and the rank of colonel is not forgotten either. Nancy is remembered as working with me in the pentagon when the subject matter was highly classified and she had top clearance . . . on top of that," with a wink at Nancy, "she's pretty too! She will keep you apprised of what is going on around you and who is thinking what . . . that you may want to respond to. Quite a team, I would say. You will be royally received and your audiences will be granted without question."

"Okay, here we are in Indianapolis, with dates in D.C. in the morning," Chris posed the situation.

"One of our shuttles will be here early and it's only moments away from the Capitol. You will wait for me to complete my oval office meeting, which will be quite short, and I'll go with you directly to the pentagon, where I'll walk behind you for effect—unless I would be required to take some action."

"And that might be . . ?" Chris asked.

"You're going to be amongst some of the most pompous, self-important, dedicated and dangerous people in the world. They represent the military might of America, and that's quite impressive—even to the Nefilim! If one or more of them go over the edge and attempt to do something destructive, they must be stopped. I would assist in doing that!"

"I'll bet that wouldn't be pretty," Don exclaimed.

"Just adequately effective, Don. No more than necessary."

Ed stood and looked at each one of his four compatriots in turn. He held out his arms to Nancy and gave her a big hug. He did the same with Jeannie. He shared a firm handshake with both Don and Chris, stood back a little and gave a most impressive yet slightly relaxed military salute. "Until tomorrow morning, then?" Ed turned and was gone.

The four were left standing, looking at the closed door. Quickly their eyes met and again Don broke the spell. "I think I need one of my marvelous martinis. Anyone?"

The conversation, the speculation and the excitement gave an entirely new meaning to the word . . . *tomorrow*.

CHAPTER
5

The morning air grew heavy with thick clouds covering most of the east coast. Though heavy with moisture, the atmosphere was brittle; people were on edge and apprehensive. Streetlights flickered off and on, traffic signals malfunctioned and the morning drive was a greater challenge than normal. Horns blared and tempers flared but Washington, D.C. was coming to life. The white house was already nervously awake.

The shuttlecraft landed noiselessly in the Rose Garden, where generations of reporters held forth. They were not there now. The entire area was devoid of people. Only marine guards stood at rigid attention, their eyes riveted on some unknown object in front of them. They came to port arms as Ed walked up the few stairs onto the porch. Ed returned the salute, each marine looking strained and tense. Inside, a marine guard led the way directly to the oval office where another guard on duty, his forehead wet with perspiration, opened the door and closed it behind Ed. Nowhere else in that part of the building was there a person to be seen.

Only three people were in the office. The president was behind his desk; the other two were tensely standing to the side awaiting Ed's arrival. Each person, the president, the vice president and the speaker of the house of representatives, stared at the man who evidently had the power to summon them. The speaker, who had been in congress for many years, was the first to break the silence.

"You're General Edwin Berkowicz! I'd know you anywhere."

"Yes I'm Ed Berkowicz . . . and I have a simple mission." All three present immediately felt the aura of ultimate authority and power. It seemed to descend like the magic cloak of Merlin to envelop the room. "Please be seated . . . Thank you. Mr. President, Madam Vice President, and Mr. Speaker; at this moment, there is a ship, a mother ship if you will, that has come from another planet to visit Earth. It is at this moment being scanned by all available detection devices and will be reported as being a mile long. Its mission is entirely peaceful. Nevertheless, you will soon get requests from the military to defend our air space with whatever it takes. You will also be advised that all military nuclear devices have been deactivated. Air strikes against the ship will be advised; you will tell the military to 'stand down' and not attack this craft in any manner."

The three looked at each other and the president opened his mouth to protest the seemingly arbitrary demand, but with one look from Ed, he closed his mouth without uttering a sound.

"You can well imagine that if this ship can get here, it can defend itself if necessary . . . with devastating effect. Simply put, the launching site of anything directed toward it will be destroyed—a terrible and needless waste of Human life. If left alone, it will continue on its way with no intent of aggression or violence. Further explanations about the ship's mission to Earth will come quickly. For now, the only course of action is to take *none*. For the good of the nation, tell the military to 'stand down' when they ask permission to strike. Do I make myself clear?"

An almost inaudible 'yes sir' was in the air when Ed bowed slightly to the three and left them with this thought: "You have noticed how the entire security staff of this complex stood aside for our visit this morning. This has been planned for some time and should signal to you how extensive our planning is. With due respect, I advise you not to do anything that would cause a peaceful and productive mission to earth to become more frightening than it need be. Mr. President, Madam Vice President, and Mr. Speaker, I wish you a good morning and an interesting life ahead." With that said, Ed snapped a precise military salute to the nation's elected leaders, turned on his heel and left the room.

In the shuttlecraft again, Chris asked him, "How did it go?"

"We'll know soon enough, but it's time for act two. Ready?"

*   *   *

The door of the shuttlecraft opened directly in front of an entrance to the pentagon seldom used except by the highest clearance personnel. As planned, Chris, Nancy and Ed were met at the door and taken by a contingent of very nervous escorts to a locked room. Identification devices were glanced at by two very serious-looking armed guards, one of whom keyed open the metal door . . . and the trio entered into chaos.

The room was huge with the appearance of a lecture hall but with many levels and balconies that were full of electronic gear and huge screens with plotting grids. On each of these screens was an image of the ship. Everyone was in military uniform except Chris and Nancy. Movement came to a standstill when they entered. Ed stood like a tower behind the two uniquely dressed emissaries. An older man, obviously in charge, approached very rapidly and spoke in an angry voice, "What the hell is going on?" He glaringly demanded of Chris. "I'm given to understand you're some kind of an expert and him," pointing to Ed, "I know."

Chris responded with steely blue eye contact, "We are witnessing a most historic event, Sir. Your satellite and radar images are correct. The object is a mother ship from another planet and it will soon be making its way slowly toward New York. It's true that your nuclear armament is disabled, as it is all over the planet. There will be no threat from another nation, as they have no capability to strike. If you haven't been told already, the President of the United States will soon tell you that no military action will be taken against the mother ship by conventional armament. The results would be most negative and result in needless loss of life. This ship is on a peaceful mission to Earth."

A junior officer came up to the older man, whispered into his ear and quickly withdrew. The older man looked up and addressed the three in precise and clipped language, "I'm Admiral Charles Rigdon. I'm charged with national defense . . . and I've just been advised the president's orders are 'to stand down' in all military responses to this invasion of our air space." The Admiral's face was quite red when he asked, "Just what in the hell am I supposed to do?"

"Nothing" was Ed's response to the question. "Just be certain that none of your staff overtly and independently disobeys the president's order. That's the extent of our purpose here this morning. Questions?"

Another man with the appearance of a scholar rather than military, walked slowly to stand beside the Admiral, his pipe in hand. "Where is this ship from?"

Ed glanced at Chris and Nancy, for them to answer. It was Nancy who spoke. "It is from the planet Nibiru, the 12th planet in our solar system, which I'm certain you have been aware of for some time." Her countenance glowed as she continued in a velvety voice, "The ship comes in peace. The people aboard the ship, many hybrids of Nefilim and Human, and many pure Nefilim will assist Humans on Earth to progress beyond the barbarism that requires military complexes like this all over the earth. Today is the beginning of a tomorrow men and women of peace have thought would never come. But it is here . . . today, and we have the opportunity of beginning a process that will change the entire planet forever, in the most positive way possible."

"National defense and situation rooms all over the globe are being visited in the same way at this time." Chris continued. "For some, it's more easily understood than here in America where UFOs and alien space ships don't officially exist. What's happening now is the wake-up call that proves they do exist and *it also proves that we are not now, nor have we ever been alone in the universe.* Again, our mission here is to prevent any mistakes from happening. I'm sure General Berkowicz made that clear."

"Gentlemen and ladies," Ed began, "I can well understand your confusion and frustration. As you well know, I worked within the politically driven military for years, both in Project Blue Book, Area 51 and Groom Lake, learning how we were kept in the dark about that which is being revealed to us now. There will be more. Please stay at your posts and wait for further orders." Ed stood at full height and brought his hand up in a formal salute. Every person in the room returned the salute, some with their mouths open in amazement, others with tears running down their cheeks. Ed led Chris and Nancy back to the shuttle.

* * *

The foul weather wasn't lost on the general assembly of the United Nations. Everything seemed in disarray. Electronic devices refused to work, lighting was off in various areas and the building seemed cooler than usual. Most delegations were in place, preparing for more discourse on the same grinding agenda. War, famine and disease were the general subjects, and there was no shortage of those who sought money and materials from the world body. As usual, most in attendance prepared themselves for another day of one-upsmanship, posturing and political speechmaking. Then a very unusual thing began to happen.

The gallery was filling with persons who seemed to materialize from nowhere. Some wore suits; some were in casual attire, both men and women, young and old. There was no idle chatter or confusion among the visitors. They simply entered the gallery and took seats as if they were waiting for something to happen!

The huge projection screen, used for all forms of audiovisual presentations, lit up with a scene of clouds rolling away from the Atlantic shoreline. Immediately, rays of light broke through the remaining fog as the sun began its journey from east to west.

A common thought appeared in the minds of all present: 'It is not the sun that makes a journey, it is the planet Earth turning in its usual rotation.' Many looked at their neighbor with the unspoken question, 'did you hear that too? Copernicus and Galileo came to the minds of most.

Voices cried out, "What is that?"

All continued to look at the screen, seeing a speck in the distance becoming larger and larger until, with the shoreline as reference, the speck had become an object so large, its shadow from the sun above it stretched for miles inland. The massive cigar-shaped object could now be seen to have rows of windows, suggesting many decks. The cylinder was perfectly smooth, unlike the Star Wars image of bolts and nuts. Its surface shimmered in the bright light with shades of iridescence that glowed with rainbow hues of all colors. Everyone in the assembly room was spellbound with this vision.

As the ship passed over the shoreline and moved inland, traffic stopped entirely while people got out of their cars and watched this spectacle. Those who could see better than others would swear that they could see people at the windows waving as they passed overhead. Their observations were correct, as they would discover later. There was no panic, no screaming and crying from those on the ground. Some got back in their cars and sat quietly. Some covered their heads with their hands in bewilderment. Most by far simply watched in awe as they heard in their heads, *"We come in peace . . . there is nothing to fear."*

The ship proceeded inland to the city of New York where all heard the same message. People soon got back into their cars and cabs to both continue to their destination or to return home. All knew this was a day unlike any other. They had seen or were looking at something from outer space; something they were told didn't exist! The new message heard by all was, "Wait quietly and you will soon learn what our mission to Earth is all about. Turn on your radios and TVs." The ship had stopped directly above the U.N. building.

The council room was full to standing room capacity. Many of the unexpected visitors were identified as scholars from all over the land, influential businesspersons, politicians and movie stars. All waited in silence while hearing, *"We come in peace, wait quietly and you will soon learn what our mission to Earth is about."*

A murmur began in the rooms behind the speaker's dais and swelled to exclamations of excitement. On to the speaker's platform walked three persons dressed in the unusual yet very sharp jumpsuit attire of the Nefilim. The tallest was Ed Berkowicz with Chris and Nancy beside him. They stopped short of the rostrum and turned expectantly toward the door they had come from.

A very tall woman of regal bearing dressed in the same attire as the other three with the exception of a golden cape draped over her shoulders, entered the room and walked gracefully to the speaker's stand. She looked over the entire assembly with a calming gaze. Her flowing dark hair shone with the radiance of a halo. She offered a breathtaking smile while raising the microphone to her level.

"I am called Sarpanit of the planet Nibiru, where the ship you have seen is from." Her voice was powerfully soft and low. She gracefully gestured to her companions on the platform, "The larger one is my son, Edwin T. Berkowicz, who is part Human and mostly Nefilim, which is the name of my people. The other two are Nancy and Chris McIver, who will play a major role in our mission to Earth." With another beautiful smile, "They are greatly Human." You could have heard a pin drop in the entire room.

"Our mission to Earth is to prepare you to take the next steps toward joining the intergalactic community. There are many other races out there, which like mine have visited earth before and will do so again when you are ready for full contact with races even more advanced than ours. This may not happen for generations but this is the beginning. Understand this, all of you are of one race, regardless of your coloration, your place of birth or beliefs. You are the Human race . . . that we, the Nefilim *created* thousands of years ago through our *intervention* in earth's development. We have often since intervened, advancing your capabilities and quickening your *evolution*.

"As you listen to me, another advance in your evolution is taking place. A part of your latent DNA is being enhanced. This is the ability to use your telepathic capabilities to better understand your fellow Humans true feelings and thoughts. This will go far in virtually eliminating deception and deceit in interpersonal relations. It will also cause a transformation within you that will dictate your honesty and forthrightness. Understand that this natural part of you will develop more slowly in some than others. The more it is resisted, the slower will be its development. The more open you become, the greater your ability will be."

A murmur began to arise in the chamber as people looked at each other with both wonder and apprehension. They were brought back to attentiveness with Sarpanit's voice.

"The ship that sits above us will continue its journey across America, stopping at selected locations, and will remain visible for a long time. We want everybody to see this beautiful craft and know that it is from another planet. The same changes you are feeling this day will be spread throughout the nation. Ships like ours are now covering the entire planet with this same mission. There will of course be confusion and social adjustments, but they are intended to be worked with, not run from. There will be political adjustments that will affect the way nations work with each other while each nation will have its own adjustments to make. This will be assisted by undoing a mistake my ancestors made several thousand years ago by confusing your language." Again that brilliant smile. "Have you noticed that there is no translation going on for you to understand what I am saying? Those of you who have headsets, take them off! No longer will any of you be deceived or misled by differences in or nuances of language. Your willingness to understand and your wanting to be understood will within a short time lead to a universal language of all Humans on earth."

Rising voices from all over the auditorium ranged from shouts of joy to exclamations of wonder. A few were sullen and staring but the vast majority had smiles and expressions of happiness. Quickly their attention returned to Sarpanit.

"There are those who will come forward to help lead you through this time of change. They are mainly

Human beings with Nefilim heritage who are receiving their wake up call to help in this time of adjustment. They have been around you and your predecessors forever and are generally known as wise persons of great integrity. They will now respond to the need for their assistance in maintaining stability. It is intended that economies and social orders will not collapse. They will continue and flourish. Constraints on creativity will disappear, allowing better and more productive ideas to surface. Competition of ideas will not be thwarted to protect the greed of others. You will be encouraged in your efforts to improve both in material matters and ideas for their implementation. The days of containing the Human spirit are gone!

"Those who subjugate others for reasons of greed and power will either change or be changed. No longer will war and its profit for the few be tolerated. New energy sources are at hand and new supplies of wealth will surface. Peoples of the world will be free of power grids, enabling them to populate more unused territories. Rather than being herded and counted, Humans can escape the crowded and unhealthy cities that oppress them and once again breathe fresh air. Then the Human race will be on course to accept those of other races that come from diverse places. This contact will allow humanity to take its place with other intergalactic neighbors. Do these prospects encourage you?"

The entire auditorium erupted with applause and shouts of agreement. The most and loudest response came from all parts of the room, asking 'how can we help?'

Again, Sarpanit's face lit up with a glowing smile that she beamed in all directions. She let the response go on for quite some time. Then, by her very posture the crowd knew to again take their seats and become quiet.

"You can all help by going back to your homes, your families and your work places. Contribute to making things better by being positive and helpful. Use your power of telepathy intelligently; have compassion for those who have less ability. It's an old saying that my son made me again aware of, 'be part of the solution, not part of the problem.' A new day has dawned for earth. You have reason to rejoice.

"Finally, there are many thousands of Nefilim that have come with me on this journey. You will know them when you see them. They are enablers, peacekeepers and all-around helpers who have been especially prepared for this mission. Ultimately, they will join with the Human race to bring upon this planet more persons like my son, born of Human and Nefilim parents. Together, you and they will be the agents of change that will transform humanity and this planet from a struggle of tribes to a true participant in the whole of time and space." Again Sarpanit offered her beautiful smile. "Thank you for coming here today. This is the first step of a long journey . . . we will take together."

Sarpanit bowed her head in courtesy, and then turned, her golden cape flowing from her shoulders as she gracefully left the podium, followed by Ed and the McIvers.

*　*　*

The great ship slowly left the UN building and proceeded southwest toward the nation's Capital. Chris and Nancy went with Sarpanit aboard the ship and were seated in the forward end to observe their progress. They were assured that all electronic media had broadcast the entire presentation to the extent of their outreach. The world had heard and seen Sarpanit, the Nefilim. She looked and talked like a Human, not some monster with frightening and bizarre features. Word spread very quickly. People were out in the streets, looking up at the ship that had come from outer space and waving with great enthusiasm.

CHAPTER
6

The hour was late in Vatican City. Cardinal Emilio Corolotti, Secretary of the Secretariat, virtual head of the Holy See, sat in the smoke-filled dimness of his private office. His ashtray was full of cigarette butts generated by chain smoking, a four-pack-a-day habit he chose not to break. The room reeked of bitter nicotine. He knew his lungs were gone, but he honestly didn't care. He was in his eighty-second year and the cancer had been confirmed. His stained finger touched "off" on his remote control . . . the TV light and sound faded into oblivion. He still wore his official robes from a day of visiting with individuals.

Two of the younger priests and one older nun had come to him separately with the vision and message they had experienced. They had each seen a huge spaceship coming to Earth from a distant planet called Nibiru, bearing people called Nefilim. Their visit would change the course of Human history. Jaded by years of deception and deceit, Corolotti was inclined to ignore the visions and prophetic insights of the countless charlatans he encountered. But this was different.

He knew about the planet Nibiru and the Nefilim from international studies and writings about the thousands of clay tablets from Mesopotamia, recently called Iraq. These three bearing the same message got his attention. These people didn't work together and were barely acquainted. He brought each one back again and was satisfied they didn't contrive to give him a false story. When he had asked his peers if they had any such experience, they all but laughed at him. Now, after seeing and hearing Sarpanit, he knew what had been foretold to him was factual. He had seen and heard—and believed.

His immediate quandary, *"Do I awaken the Holy Father now or do I wait until morning?"* His dilemma was quickly solved by a call from Guianno, the pope's personal attendant, summoning him to the pontiff's quarters. He took one last drag on his cigarette and stood up to straighten his garments. Corolotti was a small man, careful in his attire, austere in his demeanor and totally apostate. Being a well-read historian, he had long ago discarded any belief in the church's doctrine or dogma. He was only a disciplinarian, a keeper of order and a power in the Vatican to be reckoned with. He picked up his gold-rimmed glasses with the trifocal divisions and placed them in position. His eyes were watery and magnified by the heavy glass, making him look owlish and somewhat frightening.

Corolotti walked to the pope's quarters and found Guianno waiting for him at the door. "Come in, your eminence. The Holy Father awaits your presence."

Corolotti went directly to the room called the 'secluded place' with the special window in the pontifical apartment. The small window resembled the battlement openings in castle walls. It was narrow in its presentation to the outside but wide on both insides for use of weapons. In this case, it was protection from assault while still offering fresh air into aged rooms that often had the odor of their accumulated years. He took his chair with his back to the door, facing the pontiff who was waiting for him. "Are we secure?" Corolotti asked out of habit.

"The rooms were swept clean only an hour ago. No bugs!"

"You saw? "

"Yes, and understood."

The pontiff went to a cabinet and withdrew a bottle of aged brandy and two snifters. With them, he brought a pack of Corolotti's cigarettes and a book of matches in an ornate ashtray. The brandy was poured and a cigarette was lit. The two men looked at each other evenly across the table. Two old friends, who had risen in the ranks together, clicked their glasses in ritual respect for the many confidences shared in this room.

"It would appear the time of reckoning has come, Emelio."

"Why America?" Corolotti said with bitterness in his voice.

"Why not in America? It is the new Rome! It has the best, the most, the power and the marketplace. Where else would you go if you were the Nefilim?"

Corolotti drew hard on his cigarette. "We are finished, you know?"

"We were finished a long time ago, Emelio my friend. We have been the walking dead for years so far as religion goes. It's only our control of money and the unquestioning obedience of the faithful that has kept us going . . . and now that transference and obedience will slip from our grasp. This return of the Nefilim has been well designed to deny us our power over the masses. They will turn away from us quickly now. It is perceived we have misused 'the keys to the kingdom.'"

"But where will they go? Even in America, be they Catholic or Protestant, they are programmed to live by faith and belief. Who and what will they believe in? How will they be certain their souls will be saved? I thought the Americans had this thing under control. No UFOs, no aliens, nothing that didn't include chasing a ball, buying the latest fad, or believing in dear sweet Jesus," Corolotti spat out.

"I don't know the answer. I just know Mother church will be helpless to handle the inevitable questions . . . and there is no Inquisition to defend the Faith." The pope thoughtfully took another sip of brandy; "Our insistence on being the center of the universe around which everything revolves will *force* us to forgive many Copernicus's. Most will come to understand just how limited we have compelled our followers to be. Our sexually errant priests in America haven't done us any good in these past years either. Where we wink at these minor transgressions in most of the world, the Americans and their lawyers didn't. I'm surprised the church survived that challenge. This one, it will not!"

"Our wealth will survive. The banks will still control the flow of money," Corolotti defiantly challenged.

"Perhaps; we shall see. It is my fear we may no longer live in the silence where our banks are concerned. Our London counterparts will have the same . . . concerns."

* * *

Prearranged Nefilim control of all electronic media had played and replayed Sarpanit's appearance at the United Nations. The ship was making steady headway toward the west coast with shuttlecrafts coming and going regularly, delivering and returning specially trained emissaries from specific missions of contact. One such mission was to a Walter Ryerson of Kansas, Nancy's father. Ryerson was not at all surprised by the visit of a young man wearing the unique clothing of the Nefilim.

His only question was, "Are you willing to serve as a manager in your area when selected by a group of your peers?"

"Yes" was the simple answer.

The young man said, "Thank you. You will be called upon very soon." He returned to the shuttlecraft and was gone.

This scenario was repeated thousands of times over the next few hours. Chris and Nancy, aboard the mother ship, watched enthralled as the sleeping strength of the Nefilim-related population was awakened. Ed explained that this was much of his work during the last ten years and just the tip of the iceberg. There was much more to come.

*   *   *

In a portion of Los Angeles known for its gang activity, over twenty members of a gang stormed out from beneath a vacant building in full battle dress. Some wore parts of a military uniform. Others, the headscarf knotted in the back and intertwined with greasy hair. Both male and female, they were identified by their tattoos and hanging chains as one of the more vicious groups in the hood. They all carried weapons, from handguns, pipes and Molotov cocktails to simple clubs. Their attitude was sullen and more threatening than usual.

They shouted and cursed their way over several blocks to a small neighborhood business area. Most of the storefronts were boarded up but a few hardy individuals dared to stay. The only grocery store in the neighborhood was the target. The leader of the group, a tall, gaunt male wearing a perpetual sneer, walked up to the open front door and shouted for the owner to show himself. Slowly, a white-haired older man came to the door and looked out at the gang in front of his store.

"What do you want?" the owner asked, casting nervous glances at the leader and those closest to him.

"We're going to clean you out, old man. We're tired of you Jew bastards screwing us, so we're going to play Robin Hood and take what we want and give the rest to people you've screwed for years. If you don't want to get beaten to a bloody pulp or killed, get the hell out of our way . . . we're coming in!"

With that, the leader started through the door . . . and stopped in his tracks, piling up some others behind him. The owner had retreated only a few steps but was now pointing a shotgun directly at the leader's stomach.

"I'm scared as hell, but you aren't going to do this . . . not this time or any more. I've heard that things are changing and you are one of those things, like a dirty diaper that needs changing. Your kind isn't going to run things around here any more. I may die right here and now, but you might too! I'm not backing off." Waving the shotgun menacingly, "Get the hell out of here . . . now!"

The leader looked at the nervous man with his finger on the trigger and hesitated just long enough to hear the sirens down the street. The others heard them too and began to break off into smaller groups and melt away. The leader turned around and shouted at them, "You can't cut and run. We've got to stand and fight! Damn it you whores, this is our way; it's the way we live! To hell with all this talk about a new world. *This is our world.*"

By this time, the police cars were coming from both ends of the block and had the gang well boxed in. Officers poured out of their cruisers with weapons drawn and told the mostly defiant gangbangers to stop in their tracks and get on the ground. The leader, seeing that everyone decided to pack it in, pulled a pistol from his belt and turned toward the storeowner. The blast from the shotgun hit the leader full in the chest, throwing him back onto the sidewalk, dead before he hit the ground.

The storeowner immediately dropped the shotgun and fell to his knees. He looked up to see an officer coming through the door, holstering his weapon as he did so.

"I didn't want to . . . " the storeowner started to explain, his eyes wet with sincere tears of fear and sorrow, shaking uncontrollably, almost as much afraid of the police as he was of the gang.

"I know, I saw the whole thing." The officer said softly. "It was a clear matter of self-defense. He reached out his hand to help the older man stand.

"We may send someone back later to take your statement. Right now we have a bunch of jail bait out there to handle." Gesturing to the dead leader he said: "The coroner's office is on the way now to pick him up. Cause of death will be listed as 'instant death by shooting . . . while an honest man protected his property and his life." Releasing the man's hand, "Why don't you go home for a while until you can calm down? It's been a big day . . . for all of us in so many ways. We'll talk with you later . . . if we need to."

*   *   *

In Indianapolis, Don and Jeannie were up early in the morning, catching all the news stories they could find on the events of yesterday. The coffee just started to drip when Jeannie said, "Ed is back with Chris and Nancy." She went to the door just in time to see them walking down the hallway.

"Aha," Ed said with a smile. "Your receiver is working!"

"It's kind of scary, but yes! I heard you say loud and clear, we just landed and will be right down."

Chris, Nancy, and the Neals were having coffee and excitedly rehashing yesterday's events when Ed casually said to Don and Jeannie, "How would you feel about relocating to New York for a while?"

"Where in New York? I can't think of anywhere I'd want to live there! Why do you ask, Ed?" Don earnestly asked.

Chris and Nancy were silent for the moment, knowing this would be a huge decision for Don and Jeannie. Jeannie looked around the very comfortable surroundings she and Don had built over the years. "It would be awfully hard for me to leave this place Ed. I don't think anyplace in New York, even the Waldorf, could take its place."

"We discussed this before broaching the idea to you two," Ed began." We agreed it would be less of a decision for the McIvers than it would be for you. Therefore, I have an idea."

Don said quite openly, "Okay." He glanced at Jeannie who was listening intently, "I guess we're willing to hear the idea."

"Before I tell you what I have in mind, let me explain the reasons behind the proposed move." Looking at Don, Ed said: "You and Jeannie will be producing two very important things. One is the daily column on the Internet that tells stories about what is happening worldwide because the Nefilim have returned."

Don nodded agreement.

"In addition, you will be greatly responsible for writing and producing a made-for-TV special that tells the truth about how and when the Nefilim came to this planet, created the 'black-headed people' and have interacted with Humans ever since. These are two very important things you have to do."

"I didn't know about the TV thing, but it sure sounds like a good idea. Man, are the religions going to be upset over this idea," Don said.

"That's the point! They sure are . . . and will not all just lie down and roll over when their way of life is seriously challenged. They will come after you, Don."

"I know. I've thought about that . . . but accepted it as part of the deal. They've come after me before."

"But not to kill you. This time they would." Ed said with a deep concern in his voice. "They know this is the last straw in their fight to keep their cattle dumb and submissive to the old thoughts and doctrines—but the worst part is that they will be mostly undetectable when they position themselves to attack . . . *because the ones they send will actually believe they are right.*"

"My god, that sounds like Silas from the DaVinci Code."

"Exactly, Don. There are the reasons. Now, the idea!"

"I'm all for ideas not to get us killed," Jeannie said with serious enthusiasm.

"Here it is! We will go to the ship for dinner this evening and return later to your condo, just like it is

. . . only located in the U.N. building in New York. You will have a gorgeous view of the city, have all the amenities of the city and be in position where you can work . . . undisturbed."

"The U.N. building? Where is there room for us in that monstrosity—and how in the hell can you move all of this so quickly?" Don asked with proper gestures.

"The answer is *magic*. Not actually, but it would seem like magic if one were not acquainted with our capabilities. Anyway, what's wrong with a little magic in our lives? We could sure use it, and that's not all that will seem like magic as we move into the future."

"But . . . all those people in that building . . . ?" Jeannie asked.

"As we speak, that building is emptying out like rats leaving a sinking ship. Not all, mind you, but there will be plenty of room for our project. Chris and Nancy will have their quarters right down the hall. Will that work for you?" Ed asked, already knowing the answer.

Don and Jeannie looked at each other for what seemed like a few seconds only and said in unison, "Yes, It works for us." "What's for dinner?" Don asked with a smile, "What was that new vegetable?" Jeannie asked.

A mood of quiet excitement settled over five of the most important persons in America.

CHAPTER
7

Sarpanit was the first to visit the Neals condo in the U.N. building. It was prearranged by telepathy between Sarpanit and Jeannie. Don was having a little more difficulty with this ability, but it was coming along. Don had been greatly impressed with Ed on first sight but was even more impressed with Sarpanit.

"You're beautiful" came out of Don's mouth as quickly as he thought it.

"Thank you, Don." Taking Don's hand, "I have been fortunate."

Jeannie also welcomed Sarpanit with an invited hug.

"Thank you too, Jeannie. Hugging is a marvelously Human thing to do."

When Sarpanit was comfortably seated, she commented on the condo and its furnishings. "Is everything satisfactory . . . and is everything here? she asked.

"Right down to the crumbs under the toaster." Jeannie answered. "For the life of me, I can't imagine how you did it."

"In the words of my worldly son, 'no big deal.' It was easily done . . . and speaking of my son, I've taken the liberty of inviting him and the McIvers to meet with us. They will be here soon. We have a rather sensitive matter do discuss . . . all of us, especially the women."

"The name 'Sarpanit' is certainly a famous name. Were you named after the original?" Don asked.

"Yes, I was named after the spouse of my many times great grandfather, Marduk, the first-born son of Ea or Enki. I am proud of the name and the heritage."

"If I could be any one of the old ones, it would be Enki. He, more than everyone else is the savior of the Human being," Don added.

"It is true, and it is good you have this knowledge. I am proud of my many times greater grandfather also. It is he who was indeed the first true friend of

Humans, before and after the flood." Don rose and opened the door. "Ha, I got the message this time." Ed and the McIvers were right there.

When all were comfortable, Sarpanit began the conversation, somewhat hesitantly. "All over the planet . . . babies are being born that are not wanted or cared for. Some are born with terrible addictions and deformities that result from the mother's careless choices. Some are the result of rape and incest, and some are born with the HIV virus or other sexually transmitted diseases. All of this is true of America as well as other less fortunate places. We have chosen to arrest this terrible condition—but are unable to be individually selective. "Therefore, I will say it plainly, *the conception of all Human life on this planet is suspended . . . indefinitely!*"

"Oh!" Jeannie exclaimed, her hand to her throat. "That's a hard one to swallow! How? For how long?"

"For a period of several years, perhaps more." Sarpanit answered in a soft voice without taking her eyes off Jeannie.

"When Sarpanit told me of this, it gave me a sick feeling too," Nancy said directly to Jeannie. "I'm certain it will break many a young woman's heart as she struggles with her natural instinct to have children, but I have to agree. The plight of too many children is brutal and a terrible curse on humanity that must be eradicated. But there is also good news. Will you tell her, Sarpanit?"

"Yes," Sarpanit said comfortingly. "There will not be a shortage of children to raise. So many are without good homes; so many are born without hope of a home. This will change."

"You mean adoption?" Don asked. "In this country, most people can't *afford* to adopt with all the legal and bureaucratic restrictions. It's even prohibitively expensive to adopt out of the country! It's become a big money game to adopt children anywhere!"

"New leaders will have a great impact on present laws and restrictions." Sarpanit offered. "Once it's accepted that there will be no pregnancies, there will be a clamor for changes in adoption laws. It will not take long for those changes to be made when the profit and bureaucracy is taken out of the adoption business. This may be one of the most important pieces you can do on your website, the changing face of adoption."

"Following close behind is the change going on in the national legislature," Chris added. "The nation's capitol is emptying out like this building did. State legislatures are doing the same. Lawmaking is in recess and many legislators are not coming back . . .

at all! It's entirely possible that the day of the professional politician is gone. You talk about a shakeup when the real thoughts and attitudes of our esteemed leadership started coming out! *'The Emperor has no clothes on'* is now spoken out loud. First reactions to what some of our legislators really think is that too many don't! They're simply party-line parrots and next-election hopefuls! It's exactly like you have reported it many times, Don."

Sarpanit stood up and looked at every one in turn. They also stood. She took the hand of Don, then Chris and hugged both Jeannie and Nancy. She then reserved a special hug for her son, the gentle giant, Edwin T. Berkowicz. With her arm around Ed's waist, she offered her goodbye.

"The five of you and the many others who have prepared to help can handle anything that needs to be done right now. I'm going back to the ship and resume an orbit around Earth. I'll be back from time to time, but you know how mothers are; I won't be able to stay away for long, she said with a smile. "Anyway, this is Ed's project and I don't want to get in the way. He will be entirely adequate for whatever is needed here. I'll keep an eye on the progress in other nations. International trade and transportation will offer some interesting choices that must be monitored and massaged as needed."

*   *   *

When Sarpanit had gone, Don posed a gnawing question, "What about international trade? What's going to happen to the economy . . . people getting a paycheck and buying groceries?"

"First, we have to maintain order," Ed responded. "As we speak, the National Guard in all states is moving into position to quell disturbances. Looting and destroying property is not to be tolerated. The order is *shoot to kill*. This will quickly get the message out that lawlessness is not acceptable. Then, people will return to their jobs and begin making adjustments. Granted, some jobs will disappear; others will expand greatly. Believe me, we had anticipated this and have had people in place for a long time to help."

"But those who don't work, either can't or won't, what happens to them?" Chris asked.

"Social Security and pension checks will keep coming. Disability and assistance checks will continue as usual . . . pending review! Many persons collecting money they don't deserve will be culled out."

"What happens to them?" Jeannie asked.

"Survival patterns will change." Chris answered matter-of-factly.

Those who have lived on unearned or unjustified money will have a hard time, and rightly so. Those who have lived high on the hog may have to adjust their living standards. People who have lived by taking advantage of others through deceit or deception will be exposed and rebuked. And those who have virtually enslaved people through the practice of money lending will see their profits dwindle and disappear."

Nancy picked up where Chris left off. "Very clever people with very clever lawmakers in their pockets have helped create the Money Cabal that profits from virtually every transaction. This Cabal controls the private banks like our Federal Reserve and every other bank in the world. You finance a car or obtain a mortgage, they profit."

Chris continued, "New banking and lending institutions will very quickly appear all over the country. This 'new money' comes from some old money that is being donated . . . to allow its generous givers to remain in the *silence*. Other individuals who realize they have excessive amounts they will never need are also contributing. This money will be available at very low and simple interest rates that will pay mainly for its management. If you have a legitimate need or idea, you will get the money. If your new idea competes with an old idea, so much the better."

"What about the people in hock up to their eyeballs already? Any relief for them?" Jeannie asked.

"With a whole new ballgame of enforced honesty, they will work out their problems with a lender or make adjustments in their lifestyle . . . or both!" Chris answered. "Let's face it, some people just aren't too bright when it comes to taking on obligations. Couple that with the slick and sexy Madison Avenue ads, keeping up with the Jones's and 'buy now and pay later' come-ons, some people are just vulnerable. There will be real truth in lending; the wants and needs of the population will simplify.

"I can see the role of newspapers changing. Instead of competing with the Internet, they may become more local, escaping from the national agenda of the conglomerates to offer solid local information and quality advertising." Don said, "There may be fewer inane TV sitcoms separating commercials . . . maybe TV won't run 24/7 any more with all the crap they call news or entertainment! Maybe it can be used for something better than selling sex and violence and things that make kids fat."

Ed had been listening with both interest and good humor. He finally leaned forward and offered his summation.

"All of this is true, and there is more to be considered. There will be displacement and disruption in many sectors of the economy; however, it will settle rather quickly and begin an upward direction. What was intended to be a nation of laws has become a nation of lawyers. This will cease to be with the forming of a new type of court where truth and full disclosure will prevail. Legal maneuvers and tort law abuses are gone.

"The money will flow again and inevitable changes will ultimately eliminate and reduce most taxes. Governments will be greatly reduced in size and involvement in programs driven by special interests. The national debt will be eliminated through much interest being forgiven and principal paid from money not spent in the military-industrial complex. A new medium of exchange may present itself as well! Nevertheless, this and most other nations will survive and then prosper through *real* cooperation."

"I wish all the people of this nation could have heard that" Jeannie said.

"They will through Don's work . . . which begins tomorrow, Ole boy!" With a slight laugh, "I doubt he has forgotten anything that was ever said in his presence."

"I'll give it a try, Ed. Between me and Jeannie, we'll get it all."

*   *   *

Between New York and D.C., it was hard to tell which was affected the most. Each saw a mass exodus of people, going home, and just leaving. With congress virtually shut down, the law firms, the lobbyist groups and congressional staffs were left with nothing to do. Congressional leaders were at their homes and various retreats as was the president. The businesses built around their presence were seriously pondering their future.

Wall Street didn't open . . . and hardly anyone noticed! The traffic in New York was down to cabs waiting for a fare. Many of the shops were closed. Others were apprehensively open. They were few and far between.

Don, with invaluable assistance from Jeannie, crafted the That's the Way It Is story for the Internet. It contained all of the hopeful information he had received the previous day, coupled with the news that all new pregnancies would not happen and the reasons for this, but that adoption rules would be greatly revised. Both were done with extreme sensitivity, thanks to Jeannie's help. They were greatly surprised at the little response to their site. It seemed people were simply numb and in shock. They found other information linked to their site that had specific details relating to how children could be housed and adopted. It was identified by a symbol, an ancient one, that of the planet of the crossing, the winged disc, the symbol of the Nefilim.

* * *

There was no question: the United States of America was reeling from several conditions. First and foremost was the revelation of alien visitors from outer space . . . and that they came in peace. This flew in the face of the vicious propaganda about alien invaders who would kill and destroy. Secondly, the entire fabric of politically driven organization had come unraveled. Third, and not the least, there were many who didn't know where their next paycheck was coming from. How did they pay rent or mortgage; how did they buy groceries—and gas?

The first answer was that the citizens would take a holiday and the banks would not, they would remain open. Secondly, the idea was to recall the solution of the 20's and 30's when the nation went bankrupt. There was work that needed to be done in practically every sector of the nation. When there was no work to be had following the market crash of '29, the government stepped in with the CCC, WPA and other programs that built bridges, fixed roads, created parks and rebuilt aging structures. Work of this nature could still be done, but there was even more opportunity in the high-tech fields.

There was work to be done in teaching kids, recovering blighted neighborhoods, improving efforts to help those who really needed it and keeping people safe. The winding down of the vast military-industrial complex freed up people and materials that contributed to these peaceful purposes. Many great minds were turned toward real progress in research and development. With new ideas replacing the status quo and the smothering of competition, old problems were being vigorously attacked by innovation.

The money supply was adequate to meet the needs of change and growth. Some persons and families fell through the cracks but were quickly pulled out. Crime hadn't disappeared but had been greatly reduced. It just wasn't safe to cheat and steal. The great number of militarily trained men and women coming back to their homes was a real threat to those who would not renounce violence. There were more good guys who had guns, and would use them, than bad guys with guns could avoid.

Sex crimes against children, rape and murder meant removal from society . . . for good! Incarceration for these criminals was for life without pardon. Victimless crimes, substance abuse and minor offences no longer warranted being locked up in prisons. When possible, these people were turned around and included in productive society. Closely supervised work programs, educational achievement and trade training were in place quickly and well staffed. The telepathic scanning of offenders left no doubt about guilt. A badly broken criminal justice system was replaced with the criminal suppression and reclamation process, now called, the *citizens justice system*.

All of these societal changes were written about daily on Don Neal's Internet site, *That's the Way It Is*. He and Jeannie were in constant touch with Ed and other persons involved in the reconstruction process. Often they were picked up by shuttlecraft and taken to see something of particular interest. As predicted, advertising all but dried up and newspapers greatly modified their roles. Major radio and TV stations remained but with extremely truncated schedules. The emphasis was on information and education, not crass commercialism.

Chris and Nancy had become the heart of the United Nations. When countries worked at a mutual project or agreement, they were greeted by one or both of the McIvers and guided into the proper channels with the proper people. There was increasingly little of this face-to-face meeting as business and conferences were mostly conducted on interactive TV. With no language barriers and the right people speaking for their nations, the experience was exhilarating.

The same process was running governments. The president remained in the white house for the time being with key staff and support personnel. The senate and the house of representatives had not reopened . . . and no one but the wrong people missed them. It was understood that each Senator and Representative would live in the state and district they represented. They had special quarters prepared for them with staff and electronic equipment allowing them to meet with other members, hear arguments for and against bills and vote yea or nay . . . all on public TV.

However, there was little lawmaking going on. Only when someone had a progressive idea, was a bill circulated for consideration. The concept of full-time lawmakers returned to what the Founding Fathers envisioned, good people serving part time. There was to be no more legislating morals. 'One size fits all' laws and pork-barrel spending were also gone.

There were no obligatory parties, special trips or private meetings. They had a nine-to-five workday, five days a week. In the rare event that a lobbyist or special interest-group representative would visit, the meetings were open to all interested in the subject. These visits all but disappeared in a very few months. Very few of the formerly elected officials remained. Men and women who were persuaded by their peers to do the job for a limited period replaced them. The corruption of centralized and closed government was gone. Needless to say, the often suspected 'shadow government' melted away, leaving no trace except people who would now talk openly about clandestine projects. This information was widely circulated by all media.

A flat tax and national sales tax management groups replaced the IRS and other taxing entities. Without war, governmental giveaways and outright theft, surpluses abounded. The national programs that were undertaken were well funded and supervised by private groups that were fully accountable . . . and local to the problem or opportunity. The idea of having a national czar or overall head of anything seemed like a bad dream.

Finally, the idea of labor unions in any field had been abandoned. The concept of wholesome competition and fairness had replaced them. Most noticeably, in the field of education they were not missed. School had changed. Now, school was again a neighborhood enterprise. Capable parents who had obvious abilities volunteered to teach classes in reading, writing and math to anyone who wanted to learn . . . at any age.

When basic skills were accomplished and a student showed interest in any specialized study, they were initially tutored individually, then pointed to books— and helped to understand them. Many unused school buildings housed persons of need or those in transition. Don wrote a lot about education and learning.

The coming of the Nefilim had pretty well undone most religious organizations. A few diehards refused to give up their old beliefs. They were left alone. What made the big difference were the hard-hitting TV specials about the Nefilim that Don found were 'in the can' but couldn't be shown because of religious opposition. These specials were run and rerun so nobody would miss them. They started with the Nefilim coming to Earth over 430,000 years ago, eventually creating the first Human and remaining on Earth into Old Testament times. The model for these shows was taken directly from Zecharia Sitchins The *12th Planet* and the other *Earth Chronicle* books he wrote. Don had a great time being the host for the presentations. The audience was worldwide . . . and enthralled!

When the myths built around the creation epic were dispelled by solid information, the reaction was electric. With the Nefilim again amongst Humans, the myths of man-made religion collapsed. One race was discussed openly. Humans began to look at each other differently. The white, black, brown, yellow and varying hues began to make less difference. When we began to understand and accept our origin, truth and knowledge became the new religion. We were indeed brothers and sisters.

CHAPTER
8

An important event was taking place in the Vatican. Corolotti was lying in hospice, in the final stages of lung cancer. His visitor every day and evening was the pope, his friend of many years.

"Emilio Corolotti, you are dying. I feel the loss greatly. It is only you that I have trusted and listened to over the years, and now you leave me! I will be alone."

Corolotti responded the best he could, "My old friend, I welcome the worms. I am so tired. The journey has been so long."

The shrunken cadaver of a man lay before the pope, his life energy ebbing away every second, his pain dulled by welcomed drugs. This had been a man who controlled the very heart of the Vatican. He had served three popes; he knew where all the bodies were buried and the secrets of most. His passing would be the most important death in the Vatican for many years.

"Emilio Corolotti! Hear me! Before you die know this; as pope, I am releasing all prelates, priests and nuns from their vows of chastity and obedience. I am directing that all schools and teaching institutions refrain from religious training but maintain all social services. They will be open to all as learning and neighborhood centers! In the dark ages, the church was the bastion of education, knowledge. We will be known for this again in these days of change! I confess to you now, Emilio, that I too have long been aware of the Nefilim and the true origin of mankind. My responsibility was to hold the church together and maintain its—position. Now that what we denied for so long is so powerfully upon us, cannot we but be sensible? Cannot we share in the wonder of new knowledge and miracles? I may not be listened to, but I will try, Emilio."

Corolotti's eyes flickered open for a fleeting second, then closed again. He raised a thin and shrunken arm toward the pope with great effort, his fingers shaking. The pope took his hand and felt a tear of sorrow trickle down his cheek. His lips quivered when he spoke.

"Is it time, Emilio?"

A hoarse whisper came from the dying man's mouth, "Thank you, Papa. I go in peace." And with that, the arm lost its power and fell lifelessly to the bed. Emilio Corolotti had slipped into another dimension, and so had the Roman Catholic church.

CHAPTER
9

From a dark place in the Middle East, three men made their way to New York. Their mission was simple, kill the infidel Don Neal! Don had made it a practice to stroll in a small park adjacent to the U.N. building every afternoon. He had made a few acquaintances there and always welcomed their stories about how life had changed for them. These stories were incorporated into his writings every day. Jeannie always told him to be careful out there. Of course, Don always listened patiently, and did exactly as he pleased.

This day was overcast and dreary. Don had his old hat on, his collar pulled up against the chill. With hands deep in his pockets and shoulders hunched, he went through the ritual walk, his raincoat getting damper by the moment. In an instant, his senses came alive. He experienced a feeling of alarm—of danger! He looked around and didn't see anyone else. The little park was deserted.

Thinking, Mrs. Neal didn't raise any dumb kids, he headed for the barn. It was as if an alarm went off in his mind. He stopped just short of the vestibule entrance . . . and then he saw the shadows. There were two of them inside, one on each side of the door. He stopped, watching for them to make a move, then he heard the noise behind him. He whirled just in time to see a third man crumple to the ground. Then he saw Chris, his finger to his lips in a 'quiet sign.' Chris was standing close to the building, making a 'come here' signal with the same finger. Don turned toward Chris and took a few steps when he heard the other two men coming out the door. The first, then the second man went down in a heap. None of the three moved.

Building security came to the same door and immediately had the three cuffed with pipe ties, hand and foot. Nancy came out after them carrying the latest in self-defense weapons, a stun gun about the size of a cell phone. Chris had hit the third man and Nancy got the other two when they moved. They would soon reveal how they got here and who helped them. Their future was bleak.

"I don't know where you two came from, but I'm sure glad you got here", Don said sheepishly.

Jeannie came running up to them. "I've told him a dozen times not to go alone . . . but if he had to, to at least wear his Nefilim suit. Does old hard head listen to me? Heh!"

"These suits were the key to stopping the assassins. We simply stood still and blended into the walls, almost invisible." Nancy said.

"But how did you know they were here and . . . ?"

"Ed contacted me, Nancy said. He didn't say where he was but the message was quite clear and detailed. He simply said he had gotten the word from a reliable source. We moved."

"It may take some of them a little longer to civilize in their part of the world," Chris said. "When you've had kill, kill, kill mixed with mothers milk, it just doesn't change overnight . . . if at all! Let's get a cup of coffee."

*   *   *

It was going on a year now, since the Nefilim had come. World trade had resumed and general commerce was making a strong comeback. The neighborhood concept had stuck and small businesses were seen everywhere. Schooling was going along quite nicely since the Catholics, the Baptists, Methodists, most of the Faith and Belief congregations and other denominations that once preached differences, were now embracing cooperation. The schools were centers for kids and parents to both socialize and learn.

Computers in the homes were doing much of the work now. The need for being physically together in a working environment had greatly decreased, thus the need for cars had diminished. Scooters and bicycles were everywhere. The supply of fuel was not a problem.

Don's blogs were being read worldwide. Other sites had taken up the cause also and were providing useful and uplifting information daily. All sites bore the symbol of the 'winged disc.' Chris had casually remarked that Don might think about retiring to a column a week before long. Don's reaction was, "I could do that." Jeannie said, "Me too."

In all functioning media, there was an air of anticipation in the reporting, as if something was about to happen. It was in the mind of most everyone. "There's going to be a change of some kind; I can feel it!"

Nancy said thoughtfully. "We haven't seen Ed for a few days, but I can't quit thinking about him. I've got a feeling he's going to show up any minute now with something different for us."

As usual, Nancy was correct about her 'feelings.' In the mid-afternoon, Ed showed up with a huge grin on his face. "I believe we're ready for the next step in progress," Ed said. "I understand, Don, that you and Jeannie may be ready for a different type of assignment?" Ed asked.

"It's almost a 'me too' thing we've been doing, Ed. There's a lot of good work going on out there; the news is good and well reported. I do feel ready for something different."

"Then you'll get it." Ed stated emphatically. "It's been known for some time the information about contact with aliens and captured alien spacecraft was hidden from the public. Area 51, Groom Lake and S4 were all involved. Dan Catelas, a microbiologist, worked with the alien called J-ROD there. There were other aliens and their spacecraft in these complexes. Although most everybody is gone from there now, some remnants of the fantastic work done there remain. I want to show it to you!

"The American public and the world are ready for 'full disclosure,' about the secret bases, the experiments and their results. For the time being the facilities are still intact, waiting until the story can be told before being dismantled. We will have photographers for documentation, and you will supply the explanation. This will include information about how the public was deceived by the shadow governments disinformation strategy about aliens and kept in the dark about what was really going on. Ready for that new assignment? It's all yours!"

On the trip to Area 51, Ed was rather talkative about most everything except where they were going. He asked Don if he had ever heard of Dr. Pagdu of the Smithsonian. Don drew a blank and asked about him.

"He's an old friend who is not only conversant with the Sumerian culture, but his own as well, the Vedas of ancient India."

"Then he's the one Nancy worked with when she left the pentagon."

"Right; she was working with him when she met Chris."

Having heard that story, Don proceeded to his own question. "Did you have anything to do with Nancy meeting Chris in his office?"

"Of course! I found out from my mother that there's match-making in our blood. She's still at it! We're going down now."

With that pronouncement and a very slight rocking motion the shuttlecraft stopped and the door opened to reveal a huge hangar in front of them. They stepped out of the craft and walked toward the hangar.

"Pride yourself in the fact you're the only person from any form of media that has ever set foot on these grounds." Ed said with some humor.

Inside the hangar there were several strange looking types of aircraft, but nothing extraterrestrial. Ed explained, "Working from the actual ET aircraft, these are some of the results of back-engineering. Some worked and some didn't. You see, they learned from some of the Greys who cooperated in captivity . . . that's after their aircraft crashed and they survived, that the mental abilities of the Greys were involved in the operation of the craft. These mental attributes, they couldn't give to the Humans."

Back into the shuttlecraft and to Groom Lake and Papoose Site 4. Don looked in amazement at the facilities and strange-looking equipment in place. He was particularly interested in the 5 level underground structure where the J-ROD was housed, interrogated and medially treated.

Don remembered being told the movie, *Andromeda Strain*, captured the appearance of this facility. His awareness of the J-ROD, a Grey who survived an ET aircraft crash, was due to the work of James Kincaid. Kincaid interviewed a microbiologist on video. This video was widely distributed.

When the tour was over, Ed explained that the actual ET crafts had been removed and he didn't know where they were. Don was obviously overwhelmed by the shear size and scope of this mammoth complex of landing strips, buildings and hidden workplaces.

"What does this place mean to us now, Ed?"

"The main thing it means is that a rogue splinter group of our national government was able to construct and keep secret everything that went on here. It means that the American people, the congress of the United States and the executive branch were kept in the dark about both the financing and operation of this place. It also means that this black ops group, that has now virtually melted into the atmosphere, was a deadly group of people.

"If you saw something, for example like Roswell, or a retrieved alien craft and you talked about it, they discredited you, scared you off or killed you to shut you up. They were a very effective, secretive and murderous group that stayed in the dark with the excuse that mere Humans weren't ready for the truth. There are rumors that they are getting close to disclosure about our visitors from outer space . . . because their game is over. They have gone too far with their experiments. They have learned too much that they weren't ready for. Many had died or been made fools of so they could keep the secrets.

"So far as we know, they did keep their back engineering of alien craft from yielding weapons of war . . . at least they kept it from *other* war-like nations. Nevertheless, they made a mockery of the Constitution of this country, subverted every law necessary to keep operating and made it sound as if they were honorable. Hardly! Perhaps some thought about the good of this nation, but their methods of secrecy made them brutal conspirators."

"Why did you want me to see this . . . this shell of what was?"

"Simply because it represents everything our nation wasn't intended to be, secretive, manipulating and coercive. When America came about, it was to be free from religion that oppressed, free to develop individual talents and ambitions, free to express thoughts and ideas that elevated the species. This is exactly the antithesis of those ideals."

"Now that we are experiencing the Nefilim, Ed. Are there other ETs as concerned about our health and welfare as you are?" Don asked.

"No! Some are rather ambivalent about our progress . . . some are very concerned that we do not export our violent tendencies beyond our planetary environment. By and large, the other races that would contact Humankind are benign observers who are waiting to see if we can condition ourselves for contact. They don't need us; it is we who need them if we are to progress beyond our very obvious limitations."

"How long is that going to take, Ed?"

"Beyond your lifetime, Don. Perhaps beyond mine."

"So, even the longest journey begins with the first step?

"There is much that needs to be done." With that, Ed became stoically silent.

* * *

Dr. Pagdu was with Chris and Nancy when Ed and Don returned to the U.N. building. They were in a jovial mood and Jeannie had just joined them.

"Of course I know who Don Neal is," Dr. Pagdu said proudly. "I've read his columns for years and am unashamedly a fan."

"Dr. Pagdu is returning to India after forty years of living in America," Nancy explained to Don. "He has returned many times to visit and observe. Now he has been summoned by persons he respects to assist in changes that are taking place. He was about to explain when you came in."

"Yes," Dr. Pagdu picked up on the conversation; "India is a land of many inconsistencies, if you will. On one hand, we have a cadre of highly intelligent young people, many of them American educated, and who are striving for a better life. Then we have those who are trapped in tradition and overwhelmed by ancient religious inventions. . There is a priesthood that subverts efforts to free up the wonderful gift of Hinduism and accept new knowledge.

"I had just brought up the subject of the Indigo children," Pagdu continued. "They are not called that in India but rather by a very derogatory name. As here in America, they are the 'system busters' and nonconformists who seek out their own kind and change things. They are talented, very smart and not afraid of criticism." A slight smile crossed Pagdu's lips. "And many are blue eyed! In India, that is different all by itself."

"I'm surprised India hasn't progressed any further than it has." Don said.

"Much progress is lost due to very poor health condition of our people. We suffer from many diseases brought about from sick animals and rodents. We are famous for our rats, you know? Many of our beautiful temples are infested, as are our homes and businesses. These young people want to clean up this condition, but are strongly opposed by the priests and many faithful. There have been many unfortunate clashes."

"I am returning with Dr. Pagdu for a while," Ed stated firmly. "There is more going on with India than rats in temples. The Indus Valley was once the cradle of many achievements that astound us even today. Their *Vimanas* or flying machines described in the Vedas predate such things on any other part of this planet and equate to stories about UFOs worldwide. The Nefilim goddess Inanna was considerably short-changed regarding her attention to the territory the ruling council of the Nefilim assigned her.

"One look at the temples of India and you can see the influence of Inanna. She brought not only her beauty but also her brains to this part of the world. It will be my pleasure to remind India of her heritage . . . and her potential. It's been suggested that I might even assume the identity of Lord Krishna or even Lord Rama to get their attention. This I would do without hesitation . . . as has been suggested by my mother, Sarpanit."

Don and the others noticed how Ed slightly bowed his head at the mention of his mother. With some reminiscing of Nancy's days with the Smithsonian and her meeting Chris there, the meeting wound down to the departure of Ed and Dr. Pagdu. Before leaving, Ed had a special session with the Neals and the McIvers at the shuttlecraft!

"I'm leaving this one here for you." Ed declared. "You have been its passenger enough times that it has your readings encoded. You have seen it come to life when I chose to enter and it goes where I direct—*by the power of thinking it*. The craft will respond to you in the same way. I have directed it to do so. Always wear your Nefilim garments; they will protect you from unexpected occurrences. Also, the craft is your communication with me whenever necessary. Think of it as the ultimate short-wave radio. Simply enter and talk to me!" Turning to Chris, "It's not a B-2 Colonel, but it'll get you there . . . and back."

*   *   *

Ed and Pagdu set their shuttlecraft down outside a little used temple in Delhi, India. Ed wore his Nefilim garments and Pagdu was dressed like a modern Indian businessman. They stepped unnoticed from the shuttlecraft, which immediately blended into the shadowy recesses of the ornate building. As was prearranged, a limousine picked them up outside the temple and whisked them away to an auditorium where over a hundred persons were eagerly awaiting their arrival. Dr. Pagdu was greeted warmly by a small group of professional-looking men who were dressed in traditional Indian garb.

Mounting a podium, Dr. Pagdu received a standing ovation from the crowd. He motioned for their attention and, wiping a tear from his cheek, began speaking.

"Let me first introduce Mr. Edwin Berkowicz. He, more than I, will help bring about the changes we seek." When the giant of a man, dressed in what people had come to recognize as Nefilim, stood up, there was a sound of Ahhhh and Ohhh from all. Many brought their hands together before them in reverent recognition of one of high station.

Dr. Pagdu continued, "I am honored that you have invited me to come home after these many years. I return with the wish that I may assist in raising all of our people up from even the caste system we endure as Human beings." Murmurs came from the crowd and they were again silent. "I know there will be difficulty in convincing many that the changes sought are good for all. Believe me, they are, and they are necessary. We, above all people, should welcome back the Nefilim . . . and acknowledge those of the Nefilim that have been with us always, as welcome agents of progress.

"Each of you here has pledged to assist in the reforming of our society, elevating us eventually to be part of the greater intergalactic community. This will make real the Dharmas we strive for, bringing us into harmony with all Laws of Nature. This is our opportunity."

When the meeting was over, groups formed in excited conversation. A line of nine yellow robed priests, heads shaved and eyes closed, tried to weave their way through the crowd. They were blocked and turned away by some stout individuals who would not be intimidated by their presence. This was becoming a normal confrontation as the priesthood, sensing a threat to their position, began to aggressively assert themselves as disruptive opposition. Ed and Dr. Pagdu watched in silence as the situation unfolded and was handled without violence.

"Thank you for appearing with me, Ed. I'm afraid there will be more of this type of thing very soon. The priesthood has been with us since time was measured and will not give up their positions without a struggle." With a shrug of his shoulders, "Nevertheless, I must ask you to come with me to another temple where one waits to meet you."

"Oh? Who is this?" Ed asked, thinking he knew the whole agenda.

"The one your mother insists you attend. Her name is Anna."

CHAPTER
11

Dr. Pagdu stayed inside the limousine when they
arrived at the busiest, most-used ancient temple
in Delhi, saying that Anna would reunite them in due
time, whereupon he left Ed standing in front of the
temple. Children came from out of nowhere to get a
closer look at the huge man in strange clothing.
Women pulled back their veils to get a better look at
this unusual sight. Ed walked up the steps into the
temple, noticing the extreme beauty and adornment
of doors, walls and portals. The most obvious were
the depictions of beautiful women in various stages
of dress and position that graced every view. His eye
caught the carvings and reliefs above the main door

depicting the modes of transportation in ancient times. They looked exactly like modern-day flying and floating craft. This art had been in place for thousands of years.

Two elderly men in white robes met Ed as he entered the temple. They bowed and welcomed him in traditional form and motioned for him to follow them. They led him through the main hall of the building where people stopped in their tracks to stare at this stranger. He looked straight ahead and followed as bidden. He thought it strange that there were no images in his mind of where he was being led. There were no warnings, no sensory indications of what lay ahead. He thought this strange indeed.

On the second floor, they stopped at a doorway to a prayer room reserved for the highest ranking of Indian worshipers. They bade him to enter, and then melted away with bows of respect. Ed's eyes adjusted quickly, seeing a form come from the shadows directly toward him. He could not tell if it was man or woman as a cowled robe covered the form entirely. The robed figure came within four feet of Ed, into the scant but ample light, and stopped. Their minds met first. There was gentle mental probing from the robe and a gentle mental response from Ed . . . a willingness to meet was agreed upon. That was the moment Ed's life changed forever.

The figure was over six feet tall and from the initial contact, there was no doubt it was female. Ed felt there had been some kind of block to his natural abilities to sense most everything and everyone around him. Now the block was lifted and images came flooding into his mind. He stared at the still robed figure and read into a life that blossomed before him in a kaleidoscope of color and impressions.

He saw a beautiful little girl with raven black hair grow before his eyes into a beautiful woman. He felt anguish, joy and above all, compassion, love and . . . loneliness. He also felt a deep passion for life and dreams of happiness. Ed's full mental capabilities were functioning and he realized the woman before him had removed all barriers from him seeing everything she was . . . and presently is. He in return thought, how beautiful you are! He felt humbled before this wonderful person and bowed his head slightly to acknowledge her.

The figure moved closer. Two lovely arms came from beneath the garment and drew back the hood to reveal the beautiful face he had seen in his mind. Her dark eyes held him spellbound for seconds while the luxurious hair framed a face of extraordinary beauty. Her mouth was formed by slightly parted full lips that expressed openness and uncomplicated offering of herself.

Ed felt himself drawn to this woman with every emotion he had suppressed all his life. His barriers were dropping like water cascading over a high falls. He wanted to reach out and hold this woman in his arms, close to his body and close to his heart and mind. He suddenly realized *he could do this!* She was offering herself to him and he was accepting. For the first time in his life, he was shedding all fetters of self-imposed reticence and control . . . he was actually wanting this woman. The full realization of what was happening to him exploded in his mind like a burst of the sun's energy. He trembled with emotion, which for him was unheard of.

"We have met well, Ed." Anna said in a low voice, trembling with emotion. "Let us leave this place and go where we can be alone—with each other."

"Where . . . how?" Ed asked, not wanting the sound of her voice to be stilled.

A smile spread across her face revealing beautiful teeth and a glint in her eyes. "Do you not have a conveyance you can summon?"

The shuttle craft appeared as if by magic and they were borne away from the temple and directed by Anna's mind to a secluded place in the hills outside Delhi. It was Anna's own home. It was a traditional upper-caste dwelling, secluded but not without neighbors. Once inside, Anna led Ed into an enclosed courtyard with a trickling fountain, lush trees and flowers. She sat Ed on a garden bench, stepped back and shed the robe completely. Her only garment was a flowing gossamer material, which left little to the imagination. Her body was indeed as beautiful as her mind. She stood where the light allowed every contour of her curvaceous body to be seen without the immediate brashness of bare flesh.

She was proportioned beautifully; her breasts were full, rounded and firm. Her hips were shapely and full, her pleasing belly led to her genital mound of black hair with long legs accentuating its invitation. She was without adornment of any kind, no rings, makeup or painted nails. Her completeness depended only upon her uncomplicated beauty. She looked unashamed into the eyes of the man before her . . . and found total acceptance.

Ed finally found his voice. "Anna isn't the whole name, is it?"

"No. It is Inanna, but calling me Anna has been less complicated." Motioning for him to follow, Anna led Ed into a beautifully decorated room with multi-colored drapes and plush couches. She sat on the edge of one large, round ottoman-style seat and motioned for Ed to sit beside her. Ed noticed she smelled like fresh Lilies of the Valley.

"Sarpanit told me I should lead you. You have never been with a woman before, have you?"

"It is something I have often wanted—and envied of other men, but no, I have never allowed my emotions to flow as they have with you. I want you, though, and I know you want me . . . and I know it will be. It is such a strange feeling . . . and I really don't know what to do . . . with you or with myself, but I know you will show me."

"I will, not because I am so experienced but it is so natural for a woman when she is allowed to be natural. You can allow that because you are not the insecure one seeking to dominate." With that, Anna reached over and took Ed's hand and placed it on her breast. "See! I am soft and yes, very willing to love you." Anna changed her position to face Ed more fully.

"You are aware that we were prepared for each other . . . and that now the time is right that we consummate this preparation?"

"I have also been lonely and unfulfilled. Yes, I accept that the time is right."

"Can you stay with me, Ed? Can I be your companion for life?"

With little hesitation, Ed said simply, "Yes! I know you completely because you have allowed it . . . and I know that in my knowing you, I could feel you knowing me. We have nothing to keep from each other and already care deeply for each other. Yes, for you and what you believe, I know what must be, so I will say it. Inanna! I marry you! You will be my wife, my friend and my lover. Together we will pursue tomorrow and whatever lies ahead."

Anna stood up, taking Ed's hands in hers and saying, "Edwin, I marry you. I will be your wife, your friend and your lover for all time . . . and I am satisfied that our union is proper and within the laws of nature." Standing and pulling Ed to his feet, she let her covering drop to the floor. She stood before Ed entirely unclothed, smiling and glowing with excitement. "Would you like to kiss the bride?"

They lay on the bed, facing each other in a mellow twilight, sharing the lingering kisses of new lovers. Anna encouraged Ed by placing his hands on her hips, then moving so that he touched and explored her entire body with an excitement they shared. All awkwardness and hesitance on Ed's part vanished quickly and he savored the taste of her breasts. Anna moved to meet his every discovery with an eager desire of her own.

Anna was not without her own pleasure. She gently moved herself against Ed's large body and laid him on his back. With a slow and deliberate motion, she crossed his body with her leg and was astride him. Watching his face as he watched what she was doing, she carefully and slowly took his entire organ into the grasp of her barely accommodating tightness. What little pain there was vanished with the rush of excitement she felt. She had done it! She could feel the same excitement from Ed.

Anna barely moved as her body adapted to the unaccustomed invasion. Ed lay as quietly as possible, not wanting to change this glorious feeling. Then Anna began to move, almost a squirm at first. Then she moved a little up and down, raising her hips more upward each time to come down and fully recapture Ed's swollen organ. Finally she rose up, sitting erect on Ed's body, her breasts raised in sensual enticement. He rose to meet her movements, thrusting upward with his hands gripping her hips.

She felt it beginning, a thing a woman knows instinctively. Ed's body stiffened, his eyes were wide open as was his mouth. To him it felt as if every organ in his entire body was exploding with a pleasure too long denied. Anna marveled at the reality of what she had only imagined making love would be like. A slight smile crossed her lips with the realization they had consummated their togetherness and she had pleased her man. She gently moved down to lie beside him and put her arm over his chest, which was now rising and falling normally. Ed and Anna slept.

During the three days that followed, Ed and Anna experienced every sexual and mental pleasure imaginable, each learning to satisfy the other and revel in the understanding their union was a good thing. There was ample time to learn other things about each other. Anna already knew much about Ed from his mother, Sarpanit. Ed learned, among other things, that Anna was a medical doctor, trained in America at several prestigious universities, interned at major hospitals and served at a veteran's hospital in California. She had been back in India for the past five years, mainly training other physicians. He also learned that Sarpanit had been her mentor since being orphaned as a young child. Quite intentionally, Sarpanit had prepared Anna for her son.

As they lay together after a most satisfying sharing of each other's bodies, Ed said, "I must return to America soon. That is where I must continue my work." Already knowing Anna's mind, he was most pleased with her response.

"I am prepared to go with you," Anna quickly said.

"When can you leave?"

"When I was told you were coming, I knew this time would come. I have prepared. There is nothing holding me here and I am far more American than Indian. I'm sure I can be useful in America."

After saying goodbye to Dr. Pagdu, who had expected the inevitable outcome of this meeting, they left the next morning.

CHAPTER
14

The Neals and McIvers were ecstatic upon meeting Anna. It was so obvious she and Ed were in love; it was wonderful to behold. Don was most interested in the name Anna.

"Is that your full name?" was his eventual question.

"My full name is Inanna, Don. I chose not to use it when I returned to India. It still is a powerful name there that conjures up many images that were both true yet unfair in their partial truths. Inanna was indeed a great warrior, lover and antagonist. She was also dedicated to the Indus Valley and brought much of the Nefilim knowledge to a very backward conglomeration of warring tribes. These tribes eventually rivaled Egypt in many ways, as they became one people. She was far more of a leader and builder than present understanding of her allows. Of all her accomplishments, only one can I lay claim to. I'm learning to be a lover . . . of one man whom I lovingly call ET."

"Good lord, ET! Did Sarpanit plan that? Chris asked with raised eyebrows.

"It turns out that it was hers, and lately my private joke." Ed replied, "Yes, the ET was meant for what I would eventually be known as, an extraterrestrial."

"And the name Berkowicz? Don asked.

"Edwin Theodore Berkowicz, a name once learned, seldom forgotten. Useful for a major general in the U.S. Air force, but chosen at random for that purpose. I never have known my father's name. Unfortunately, it makes no difference. Sarpanit would have loved only a good man."

"Here's something that may make a difference," Jeannie said as she reentered the room holding a page from the printer. "It seems the executive wing of the white house is vacated. The president has stepped down, the vice president had already resigned and the speaker is gone also. The exodus from D.C. is continuing en masse. It's expected D.C. will become close to a ghost town in the near future."

"It's also expected there will be a new location for some form of central government, located near the center of the country," Ed offered. "I doubt there will ever be another single leader or the old form of representative democracy."

"What will government look like, Ed?" Don asked. "Do you think Americans are ready to write off the constitution and our national heritage?"

"I'm afraid the constitution died on the operating table long ago, Don. Politicians and lawyers, often one and the same, carved on it until it bled to death. It, like the commandments to the ancient Israelites, The Magna Carta and similar efforts to regulate Human behavior, have all passed away in their entirety. Remnants of each remain in their intent, but all things change. The Founding Fathers of this great nation did an outstanding job in creating a workable document; but how could they have known the size and complexity of what we've become? How could they have foretold the political breakdown of the representative democracy they devised? They were warned that the Republic would be hard to keep. Mr. Franklin was correct. As Thomas Paine said in *Common Sense*, in 1776, *"We have it in our power to start the world again,"* only this time we'll do it right so that it doesn't have to be done again. Now is the time to vacate the old and build the new.

"Speaking of vacating," Chris began, "this building is about totally empty now. I don't know what's keeping it running, but it can't be for long."

"We're keeping it running," Ed said matter-of-factly. "The Nefilim inserted a power source to keep the necessary parts of this old structure going."

"What kind of power source?" Chris asked with keen interest.

"Several forms that will soon be available to all people who will use it properly," Ed responded.

"Properly?" Jeannie questioned.

"As it is used for productive applications only. It cannot be weaponized; it will be individualized like your Nefilim garments. You have seen that you are neither too hot nor too cold regardless of atmospheric conditions while wearing this clothing? The clothing and the person become as one. This is one power source that will become available to all who progress in their mental capabilities and will be earned by learning true ways of righteous living."

"I know that sounds like a religious enticement, but it is not," Anna interjected. "Righteousness and religion have nothing to do with each other, they never did. True righteousness means that the evils of lust, anger and greed have been overcome as one becomes more enlightened."

Ed continued, "Another power source will operate mechanical requirements. America and other nations are rapidly approaching a rebirth of all things that made them great. The stores of carbon based fuel are rapidly diminishing in America and worldwide. The reserves of stored food and water are also running out. Of course, business and industry must recover and is poised to do so . . . and we have proper and adequate energy sources. We will make these sources available.

"Once again, we all will play a pivotal role in getting this started. Anna and I will team with Nefilim medical people to revolutionize healing the sick and injured. Chris, you and Nancy will be able to assist in the recreation of a national government. Jeannie and Don are free to go wherever they choose and report on progress with an ever-expanding internet." With a slight smile, "They may even contribute to some print media . . . that seems to have more than nine lives."

"With all of this in mind," Nancy picked up where Ed left off, "We have received a special invitation from a very special man in Kansas, my father! He has thousands of acres that lie fallow and would be the ideal location for the development of a seat of government . . . and also good for us. Anybody up to leaving this place and starting our own community?

CHAPTER
13

It's the end of year three since the coming of the Nefilim. Profound changes they brought and implemented have firmly taken hold. Once again, America is an agrarian nation. Once again, the productive citizen is in charge. Many of the older and larger cities have been melted down to usable parts and are virtually uninhabited. Huge tracts of land within the old mega-population boundaries have been reclaimed as farmland and green space. Portions of suburbs remain as centers of population but with drastically changed dwelling places. Function and utility have replaced grandeur and opulence.

Many of the previously uninhabited parts of the nation are now teeming with Human life. The most fundamental change is in the attitude of the people. Extended families are again the way of life. The very old live with the in between and very young. Once again, there is a feeling of continuity in living with a sharing of values and experiences. Respect for elders is returning as the young experience their older family members ability to teach and encourage.

Children are again valued and cherished; there are no orphanages. Raising and instructing the young is once again a community effort. The value of the young is fully recognized, with discipline and care meted out in equal parts. There have been no Human births on planet Earth since the Nefilim came. There is no Human life on the planet under three years of age.

Allowing nature to take its course, birds of a feather have flocked together! With the decision of governing bodies to be less concerned with most borders and boundaries on the North American continent, ethnic groups have drifted together and are prospering. Forced integration has become unthinkable, but Humans of like values and desires have found each other, regardless of their color, size or age. There is much movement within and between such communities as values and desires change. New ideas are usually welcome but overly aggressive behavior is unacceptable. Misfits and troublemakers soon move on or are moved on. They soon understand they must change or there will be no place for them—in this world. The initial gift of the Nefilim, the virtual elimination of deception and deceit, has transformed the way Humans interact.

The Nefilim have shared their medical skills and healing abilities with great benefit to the general welfare. The elimination of language separation has allowed an understanding of individuals and their abilities that contributes to a growing interaction of exploding progress in living dynamics. The energy sources the Nefilim have shared make all the difference in how Humans live . . . separately and together.

All of these things that are changing the North American continent are changing the other landmasses as well. Two changes of incalculable value are allowing all of this to succeed. One is the motto of planet Earth, *"The Human race is all one species. Our coloration and stature make us individual, but we are all one family meant to live in peace."* The other is the complete elimination of man-made religion. With the coming of the Nefilim and the realization of our true origin, there is no need to fabricate fairy tales or invent and reinvent gods.

When it was generally realized and accepted that virtually all wars are both caused and fueled by religion, religion quickly faded from the Human psyche. Further, when it was realized that religion was used by groups that sought to gain power and wealth for themselves by initiating and then financing these wars, these groups were exposed and dispersed. Many of these groups were the very religious organizations that sought to control their adherents through fear and deception. They no longer exist.

When survival and rebuilding a society were more than full-time jobs, many things changed in the daily lives of Humans. Advertising schemes and selling by sexual exploitation disappeared. Chasing a ball again became a pastime of fun and relaxation rather than a multi-billion dollar obsession. There was little time for escapism when food, clothing and shelter were on every day's menu. Simplify and make good was the continual effort.

The moral fiber of humanity had undergone a badly needed upgrade during the past three years. The inability to hide behind legal gymnastics of defenses when a crime was committed changed society. With deception and deceit virtually impossible, an offender was quickly known and dealt with. Prisons warehoused the incorrigible and unrepentant;

conclusively proven rapists and murderers were quickly executed. Rehabilitating the criminal most often succeeded because crime was simply not tolerated. Marriage again became a family matter only and was simply announced. Rarely did a marriage dissolve. When one did, it was handled by the families, not outsiders.

With no replacement life being born and the elderly dying when their time came, the population of the planet had begun to shrink. Health care had undergone a sea change with the Nefilim returning. The population was now healthier and stronger, reminiscent of the frontier days without the hazard and disease that claimed many of that day. It was only natural that woman again yearned for her own child to raise, to make a family of her own and watch it grow. There was a rising sentiment that this should be again allowed. By now, though, most understood that there should be no Human births contaminated by disease or addiction. There were enough unwanted and unloved children available to satisfy the need of men and women wanting a family.

These are the basic conditions found on the North American continent at the beginning of year four of the Nefilim's return. Conditions were similar everywhere, even in the most backward and violent regions.

It was the absence of religious differences and the understanding of being one race . . . Human, that made this possible.

Most of the pure Nefilim had left the North American continent by this time. Of the thousands that had come and gone, there remained few. However, the entities like Ed Berkowicz who had awakened to their Nefilim heritage were legion. As foretold, they had emerged from all walks of life to assume leadership positions they had previously scorned or avoided. They were the new "Men and Women of Renown." They and other capable and advanced Humans were in charge. It was fascinating to watch as the Nefilim would take center stage in a group of people and simply stand there.

You could feel the power emanating from the Nefilim as they stood strong and tall, waiting for individuals to feel the call . . . and then they came. One by one, they stood before the Nefilim and were touched on the forehead by the hand of the Nefilim. They simply turned and walked away from the crowd as an awakened entity. They were soon in the mainstream of progressive change. A new leader or a strong follower was born in that simple ritual.

Ed and Anna had succeeded in developing healing centers in most communities. The large and often deadly buildings called hospitals were no longer necessary. New and less toxic medications now treated a wide variety of diseases that plague the Human body.

Diagnosis was accomplished by body scanning technology with suggested treatment resulting. Most all surgeries were performed by nano-tech laser and, with rapidly healing medications, seldom required much down time. Thousands of medical staff had been trained for specific procedures. "Healer" replaced the designation "Doctor" and many were called to this service.

Don and Jeannie continued to produce their special communications for the Internet, working from their home back in Indianapolis, IN. Their condo went the direction of most big cages for Humans. They now have a small bungalow adjacent to the grounds of Butler University, a now thriving community of artists and writers who contribute to general public education in its various forms.

Chris and Nancy remained close to the new governmental facilities in Kansas to help hone a completely new process of governance. Walt Ryerson, Nancy's father, had reluctantly accepted the position as president, or chairman of the council. He proved to be an able leader. He formed a superior template for further development of government of and for the people.

The government buildings in Kansas were all three stories or less and were interconnected. Acting president Walt Ryerson had been quite specific about certain aspects of the buildings. First, their construction was such that they were as tornado proofed as possible. Living quarters for the necessary staff were not quite Spartan but were simple and functional for singles as well as families. Long stays were not anticipated.

America had learned the hard way that neither public servants nor politicians benefited the nation through long experience on the job. Incumbency in any governmental office had been eliminated; civil servants like all staff were rotated regularly. The adequate compensation and growing respect for the various positions yielded a cadre of willing and competent persons to serve. Those completing a one or two year stint in rebuilding the national trust were greeted as true heroes when they returned to their communities.

The offices were quite similar to preNefilim times with a president, a vice president and the various cabinet offices. The difference was the elimination of political parties and the way each office was filled. Campaign money raised and old family connections were no longer a consideration. With the absence of deception and deceit as political tools, a completely different type and set of candidates presented themselves for interview by a select council of twelve. This council was comprised of six Humans and six Nefilim, equally divided by six females and six males. The interviews were open to all on the Internet. These interviews were polite and open, seeking only to determine who had the best ideas of how opportunities and objectives could be approached.

Increasingly every day, men and women who were proven entities in the management world of old America and were known for their basic decency and ethical practices were coming forward. Where the bitterness of partisan politics and governmental excesses had prevented it in the past, good and capable people were now willing to assist for a while, in local and planetary management. Now that religious agendas were gone as were race and gender, the only questions posed were regarding the welfare of all the people.

Each state or province had its committee of twelve. With political gerrymandering a thing of the past, each geometric district within a state or province had one representative. This representative was required to live within the district he or she represented. This representative went to work every day at a specifically provided facility. This facility was comprised of conference rooms and a general meeting room that resembled a university lecture hall. In the center of this public room, TV monitors were set up for all to see and hear whatever governmental business was at hand. The gallery was open to the general public.

Whether it was local or global considerations, all conversations were open for public scrutiny. The representative's job was to receive input from all quarters of his or her district and be guided by its content. The ultimate result was majority rule or a compromise within that district. There were no trade-offs or deals made in closed rooms. Simple geography and transparent processes had eliminated government and corporate lobbyists. Each district ultimately developed its position on questions both local and global. The local positions were implemented immediately and positions on other than local situations were passed on to Kansas for general consideration and further guidance.

Referendum was the means of voting on all situations requiring a vote. It was all accomplished electronically and a vote could be cast from home on a computer. Social security numbers were now used exclusively for the identification of voters. The illusion that everybody didn't have a number was quickly dashed and the reality was used to perpetuate the modified democratic republic. If one was a contributing member of any community, they had a number for voting, and of course, all other matters requiring identification. This number was forfeited only in extreme cases of discipline or punishment. This could come quickly from wrongful use of the assigned number.

"One man, one vote" was still accepted as reasonable. If you were a contributing member of society, you would not be denied that 'one' vote. However, if a person was certified by a learning center to be able to read, write, and perform basic math functions, that person was awarded the second vote. The third vote was given for community service. A good number had been awarded already.

This voting change had proved an incentive to many previously unmotivated individuals to learn the skills necessary to have more than one vote. There was justifiable pride in being a multiple voter. One was recognized as a leader and good citizen, regardless of color, size or gender. Participation in the voting process was over ninety percent

*   *   *

Ed picked Don Neal up in Indianapolis in his shuttle craft for one of their many trips throughout the country to see another innovation contributing to an ever-expanding economic recovery. Their destination was the area of North Carolina, Kentucky and Tennessee where, as many others were, their economy depended upon the sale of tobacco.

"You mean there are no more tobacco crops at all?" Don asked incredulously.

"Correct." Ed replied in his usual brief way.

"Then what the hell are they going to live on?"

"That's what we're going to see, ole boy." Ed replied with the quick smile he had acquired with the advent of Anna in his life. "It's time to write the story, and of course you're the man to do it."

Ed and Don sat their craft down on several sites and talked to the enthusiastic people working the farms. Most had been born and raised on the farms and knew great changes were coming because of the proven health hazards tobacco represented. They were overjoyed at the way their changes had come. Several major questions had been answered that allowed these changes. These were the facts Don was gathering information to report. Within just a few hours, Don had what he needed and proceeded to write his now weekly column for the Internet. The following is a portion of Don's report:

When I was young, like many others, I smoked. Cigarettes were cool to do and the movies glamorized them in the lips of tough guys and lovers alike. They cost about twenty-five cents a pack and I always wanted to look like the Marlboro Man. As years went on, filters were touted as the answer to people getting sick from smoking. I did filters. More years passed and the price per pack went up, the government had glommed onto tax revenue from their sales . . . and people kept getting sick . . . and dying. Before the Nefilim came and smoking was eliminated totally, the price per pack was outrageous, tax revenue for the government was huge . . . and it was proven conclusively that smoking kills the Human animal. Nontheless, the unholy alliance between the dollar and nicotine continued.

The elimination of smoking was tough for many who were addicted to the nicotine . . . and the tax revenues. With the help of a withdrawal treatment the Nefilim brought, the habit rapidly diminished, but people still died from many years of abuse to their bodies. Many were able to quit and reduce their damage from smoking and were healthier. Tax revenues from the sale of tobacco were not greatly missed . . . mainly because there was no congressional fund-raising group called the IRS to collect them. But the people who depended on tobacco as a crop for a living? They had a problem!

Most tobacco farmers raised other crops as well, but their main revenue was from the tobacco. It was looking as if they were in a world of hurt. The Nefilim brought an answer to the dilemma. They had anticipated this problem and had a *ready-made solution that helped solve two problems. Remember, it was the Nefilim who brought the grains and many new plants to planet earth thousands of years ago. This time, they brought a very special grain that solved two problems.*

It was a grain very similar to corn, could grow in the soil that had known only tobacco forever. It was hardy and could often produce two crops per year. Most importantly, the crop produced a harvest of kernels that easily yielded an ethanol-type product to fuel internal combustion engines. These old engines are still needed until the Nefilim's energy sources can be totally implemented. It's the best of both worlds, like 'making lemonade out of lemons.' The day of fossil fuel pollution and non-renewable energy sources is at an end. General use and renewable energy sources for all is the next big story! It's coming! That's how it is.

—Don Neal

*   *   *

Ed and Chris found themselves on the outside of the conversation when Nancy and Anna were caught up in a conversation with several other women centered on food preparation. Although interested in food itself, they soon found themselves sitting in a quiet courtyard, looking out over the flat landscape as the sun sank lower into its daily retreat.

"What happened to us, Ed?" Chris asked. "How did we Americans become so lost in our pursuit of life, liberty and happiness?"

Ed remained silent until the sun had practically disappeared and the long shadows became a beautiful twilight. Chris had almost given up on an answer, when Ed said simply, "About the same way the Nefilim lost their way on Earth many thousands of years ago . . . the illnesses of jealousy, greed and avarice. My forefathers, particularly Enlil and Enki with their hatreds and fears of each other, warred with each other and eventually brought Humans into the war with them. Add to that the genetic imperative that was programmed into the Human to serve gods, and there you have it. War and religion! The two curses of mankind that feed on each other and eventually destroy us."

"Both followed us from Europe, Ed, and it seemed they were contained . . . !"

"Until the war for independence from England . . . until the war against the American Indian . . . and then the Civil War against ourselves! Then the great world wars that would end all wars. Then the political wars that raged right up to the day the Nefilim came. And think of it! Just about everybody involved in these wars claimed to worship the same God. You know, the one that has come to micro-manage so many people's day-to-day lives. The same one we have adopted and adapted from the ancient Israelites. Man has made and remade this God too many times."

"Tragically true, Ed."

"Indeed tragic, Chris."

"Things are certainly changed now." Chris offered after a few moments of thoughtful silence, "Where do we go from here?"

"America and most of the developed countries have handled the last three years pretty well. There's much to do, but we have accomplished much. Some individuals and groups of persons that refuse to accept the changes taking place or continue in their violent ways fueled by irreconcilable hatreds must be dealt with."

"How?"

"They will be identified, reasoned with and evaluated as to their rehabilitation prospects. If it's determined they are indigestible, they will be separated from the rest of Humanity . . . permanently."

"A 'devil's island' situation?"

"A little more humane, but yes, a total separation that removes them from us and lets them live out their lives with people of similar choices. They will know what their sentence will be if they don't shape up . . . and there is no deception or deceit possible."

Chris could barely make out Ed's face in the gathering darkness. His mind raced with the possibilities for the future. He had known many of the types Ed referred to over the years in and out of the military. "Permanently separated, not killed, but separated to live out their lives as best they could. We would no longer 'warehouse' these people, but rather contain them. A logical solution."

Ed, apparently reading into Chris's thoughts, said, "Yes, Chris. A logical and needed solution."

"What have you two been doing? Solving the problems of the world?" Nancy said, being followed closely by Anna.

"We're working on it as usual." Ed replied with a hint of humor in his voice. "Any great new dishes we'll be seeing soon?" Chris asked.

"Just us again," Anna chimed in. "We're all the new dishes you can handle."

"Amen." Chris breathed loudly.

"One of the ladies we were talking with had just come in from Washington D.C. She said the place is immaculate and doing its job as a Museum of History for America," Nancy offered.

"Haven't seen it for almost three years now," Chris said, "What's it like?"

Anna set a small lighted candle on the table near them, which added a soft glow to the mild Kansas evening. "Do you realize we can sit here and enjoy each other without being afraid of some kind of criminal violence? That had become almost impossible in D.C. . . . and most other parts of the world. We have come a long way."

Nancy picked up on her report. "The homeless now have homes again . . . and are some of the strongest contributors to the upkeep of the monuments and streets. They now occupy space previously reserved for the huge bureaucracy. The parks and all greenways are well kept; there is no litter and no crime. People are again coming from everywhere to see what was the capital of America. The white house and congressional houses are big on the list, and most of all, The Smithsonian museum is fully intact and open to the public."

"Did she mention Arlington national cemetery?" Ed asked.

"She certainly did," Nancy replied. "The elite honor guard maintains its perpetual vigilance at the tombs and gravesites. It is also still meticulously maintained and heavily visited."

"It is now more than ever honored as a memorial to those who served . . . and died for their service." Chris added. "While we try to forget war, we mustn't forget those who couldn't forget it."

Ed simply nodded his head, his eyes closed with many memories that had faces and names. "It is good that it remains." He said with a deep sadness in his voice, "We need to remember."

The four sat in silence for several minutes. Chris was the first to speak. "What happens now, Ed?"

"For three years, the other races in the galaxy have made few appearances in Earth's skies. This will begin to change as their airships will show themselves . . . in greater numbers and in selected places. In America, we will begin the process of contact quite soon."

"Are we ready"? Nancy asked.

"We're ready to begin!" Ed replied. "We will begin to discuss with the others when we can fully integrate Nefilim power sources into America's growing capabilities and when there can be contact with the other races. Some can assume our form; some will refuse to do that, and they will appear quite different. So be it! It has been shown rather conclusively that the Nefilim and the Human can live together in peace . . . and a great deal more than that, in harmony . . . even love! Yes, we're ready to begin a process that will bring planet Earth into the Galactic Federation."

CHAPTER
14

There was no moon to shed its light over the Carpathian Mountains in Romania. The craggy mountain peaks were enshrouded in the night mists which enhanced their storied mystique. From the dawn of recorded history these mountains and the peasants who made them their ancestral home were said to be touched with most things evil and reeking of death. Nothing had changed on this night.

The unrest of the goats and other animals had awakened a young peasant boy. He responded sleepily to the unusual disturbances in the pens, followed closely by his younger sister. She was fifteen and he had just turned seventeen. Their mother had died the year before of an illness that took all of her breath. Their father was down in the small town at the foothills of the mountain where they made their meager living by gathering roots and raising goats.

The strange lights in the highest parts of the mountain had been gone for about three years, and the terrible stories about people being stunned and carried off to have small creatures with big eyes examine them, often painfully, were hardly forgotten. It was always the same people who claimed to be taken; men, women and children of both sexes. Sometimes the children didn't return and the parents couldn't remember what had happened to them, much less make others believe them. This had been going on for about thirty years, but no one would speak of it. When the subject of 'being taken' was brought up, heads would hang with eyes downcast and the sign of the cross repeatedly being given.

This night, two young people stood and watched streak after streak of light being swallowed up by the mountain darkness. In the town below, from the tavern men looked up toward the mountain, seeing the same streaks of light disappearing into the darkness. They remembered the troubles of years ago, shuttered the windows and drew the bar across the door. They sat in silence, the brew dulling their painful memories. The father of the two youngsters sat in his own silence, convincing himself his two children would not venture out into the night. "Sure, they'll be all right."

*   *   *

The bright light blinded both the boy and his sister. The beams caught each separately and they were taken off their feet, unable to move or resist. The boy saw his sister being taken into a rounded object that pulsated with flashing lights. He followed behind her. His clothes were all removed and he lay helpless on his back with several strange and frightening creatures looking at him with large black eyes, their long, bony fingers touching him all over.

From the corner of his eye, he could see his sister in the same condition, naked, on her back and head turned toward him with eyes closed, her mouth loosely open. Her arms hung limply down from the flat surface she lay upon. His first thought was, 'she's dead!' He saw the bright ball-like object descend from somewhere above her and a thin, bright light begin at her chest and slowly move down her body.

He then realized the same thing was happening to him . . . he felt the first shot of pain as he looked down toward his own chest. The light seared and cut his flesh and he could smell the acrid burning odor. The full pain arrived as a rolling thunder that became louder and louder until it was a deafening roar. He tried to scream out in agony but found he was falling into a darkness that turned black. His life force ceased to exist and his scream was not heard.

* * *

"What is it Ed, "Anna rose up in their bed and saw Ed at the window, his huge frame hunched over looking out into the Kansas night.

"They've returned Anna, the Greys have come back. I can feel it."

"I thought they were gone for good . . . I thought the Nefilim had banished them from the Earth!"

"I was not told so," Ed said with anger in his voice. He turned to face the frightened look on Anna's face. "I assumed, and I was wrong. Come! Dress quickly in full Nefilim clothing. This will be a long and disturbing day . . . or many days!"

* * *

In a small community close to the Missouri River, Clyde and Betty were sound asleep when their sleeping room was flooded with light. They awakened to find the room crowded with the same small gray creatures they had encountered many times. It had been over seven years since they were last taken aboard alien ships and examined like laboratory animals. They both still bore the scars, both physical and mental, from these episodes that began early in their married life. They were now in their late forties.

The same fear was there, a little dulled from their many experiences, but none the less, a sickening fear that preceded the numbing paralysis that engulfed them. They had reported the previous experiences to the authorities. They had been interviewed and tested. They had agreed to regression hypnosis to recall their experience. They had co-operated in all ways with a myriad of officials and interested parties they encountered. After the same thing happened several times, no one would listen anymore. They became a voice crying out in the darkness that no one wanted to hear. It became painfully obvious that UFOs and little gray men didn't exist—in the United States of America.

This time was different. There wasn't the careful handling and curious probing. This time, they were stripped bare and placed on their backs in full view of each other. Where before, needles and soft probes entered their bodies with some care, this time they both saw the beam of light burn into them, and open them up like a hog would be butchered. They only saw and felt the beginning of this process because their bodies and lives were now expendable . . . and they were quickly dead.

*   *   *

In Russia, Japan, Australia, and Italy, the incidents were the same, with one difference. The bodies were being found, often many miles from where they were determined to be taken from. The hideous wounds were basically the same. They were slit open by a precision tool thought to be a laser of some sort that cauterized as it cut . . . from just below the sternum, down through the pelvic bone. All of the organs of reproduction and elimination were gone—surgically removed with great precision. Both men and women were the victims. There were no small children taken.

*   *   *

Nancy's greatly increased ability to hear and sense what wasn't said caused her to waken Chris.

"There's something happening, Chris. Ed is talking with his mother, Sarpanit and there is both confusion and anger involved. We are under some kind of attack from the Greys."

Chris and Nancy were soon in the common room of their adjoined compound with Anna saying Ed would be right there. "There is to be a meeting in the Mother Ship immediately," Anna said. "You have the option to attend or not attend."

Ed came into the room, his face flushed and his features dark. "I knew you would choose to go." He said to Chris and Nancy, "Good! This will be a very different experience for all of us. Come, we will take our shuttle."

The shuttle stood waiting in its special place, the door open. Chris and Nancy went aboard first, followed by Anna then Ed. The command was given and within minutes they were inside the mother ship. They were met by a young Nefilim woman who led them to a meeting room directly behind the ship's bridge. Sarpanit stood waiting for them at the head of an oblong table. She motioned Ed and Anna to her right side and the McIvers to the other.

A screen at the far end of the room lit up with images of the beings called "Greys." They were around four and a half feet tall, large heads with the often pictured large black eyes and small mouth. They were slender with tapered limbs and tentacles like fingers. They displayed no signs of sexuality but appeared smooth, like the skin of a dolphin or other sea creature. Their eyes captivated you, like the black, unfeeling eyes of a shark just before he rips a piece of flesh from your body.

The images on the Internet screen changed to very graphic pictures of the recent victims. Everyone was virtually gutted and died with their eyes open, their mouths in the form of a grimace or a scream. From the various positions their bodies had assumed, it was evident they were hastily discarded as unwanted garbage. Reports were flooding in from all parts of the planet of more bodies found. It was pandemic, worldwide pandemic.

The door to the room slid noiselessly open and three figures appeared. The first in was immediately recognized as a Grey. He glanced at the screen and awkwardly proceeded to sit down at the far end of the table. He showed no emotion nor did he make any noise. He simply sat down as if it were an unusual position for him to take. The other two were taller and heavier. They wore robes of shimmering satin material and were greeted by Sarpanit's gentle nod of welcome and recognition. Sarpanit said, "The first to enter is a Grey who recognizes the error of his race and will work with us to end the problem. The others are Zeta. They are our allies and will work with us to end the menace of the predatory Greys.

Where the Grey made no indication of recognition, the Zeta returned Sarpanit's greeting and gestured in kind. Their faces were rounder, the mouths more pronounced and the eyes, though still black, were less threatening. They soon learned that the Grey sat at the far end of the room to protect the others from the stench he carried. Their olfactory glands soon adapted, but the smell was persistent. The Zeta seemed not to be bothered by the odor.

Sarpanit spoke to Chris and Nancy directly. "The Zeta and Greys do not communicate vocally. All contact is by telepathy and may be difficult at first. You will soon have no difficulty . . . and by the way, thank you for coming."

Chris and Nancy sat transfixed by what they were seeing. These were actual aliens . . . beings from elsewhere . . . other than Earth. They were making contact with aliens . . . real ones. Chris was the first to respond to Sarpanit, and he did so telepathically. "Thank you for inviting us, Sarpanit. We are honored to be with you and Ed at this time."

Sarpanit asked of the Zeta, "What is happening?"

The sound that came to Chris and Nancy's ears was at first low and blurred, but quickly cleared and became audible. Each glanced at the other with recognition they were hearing the same.

The Zeta's mouths didn't move but you could tell which one was speaking by slight gestures each would make when communicating.

" . . . we welcome our brother Grey, as you call them, and remind you that they are a part of our race that strayed long ago from our ways and are now facing extinction—unless they can somehow blend the life particles you call DNA into their genome and recapture the vitality needed to reproduce. They are without replacement in their society. They are not welcome back into ours.

"They insisted cloning was the answer to perfection in the race and certain of them broke away from our society to form their own way of life. Now, they are all clones, without a life particle supply to revitalize themselves . . . and their DNA has deteriorated. They prey on Humans to recapture what they need to save the race."

"How can we stop this carnage of the Human on planet Earth?" Sarpanit asked.

"You cannot. We must do it." the Zeta replied.

"Why is the Grey here with us?" Ed asked.

"To carry the message of what we decide. He will not communicate with you as he is ashamed but he refuses to acknowledge that to you. He is ready to die, which he will most certainly do, when he returns to his kind. They will kill the messenger."

"Are we bargaining?" Sarpanit asked.

"In good faith we trust . . . this time in good faith!"

"We understand the Zeta and the Grey have been in touch with Humans who have deceived you!" Sarpanit stated.

"Their words and agreements to us were similar to those given to the Native Americans when America was growing. One treaty after another, one lie after another, and finally we gave up. But it is the Greys that return with a vengeance. The leaders you sent to work with us cannot be trusted, and now the Greys are out of control."

"They were not true leaders of America or the planet. They were power-hungry opportunists who now are exposed and disposed of." Ed replied.

"Not all have been found," The Zeta stated.

"You mean there are still some we have not uncovered?" Sarpanet half rose from her chair as she spoke.

"There are several, kept hostage by the Greys and thought to be a bargaining chip when the time was right," the Zeta answered.

"They are of no value to us," Ed answered quickly. They can be disposed of with no loss to the planet."

"We cannot do this ourselves," the Zeta exclaimed. "We will not take the life of a Human . . . but the Greys can . . . and as you see, they will do without guilt."

Both Zetas turned toward the Grey. The Grey simply nodded his head.

"What do you want of us to stop the killing?" Sarpanit asked quietly.

"Can you speak for the Humans on planet Earth?" The Zeta asked.

"I can," Ed replied. "Earth is my mission, given me by the Nefilim. Within reason, I can speak for the Human race . . . and Sarpanit will speak for the Nefilim. What do you want of us?"

"We want to be the first to contact Humans as a race, apart from them, yet to be accepted and trusted to share the planet in peace. There are not many of us who would come, fewer than your count of a thousand, and it will be fewer when the . . . terrors are eliminated. There will not be many of us left in this dimension."

"Why is that?" Chris asked.

The Zeta answered, "When it is determined there is no other path but to kill, those who kill must perish with that one who is killed. Killing is simply killing and cannot go unpunished. It is the law of the universe."

"How will you direct this . . . killing?" Nancy asked.

"We will not direct it, we will lead it . . . and we will die. It is understood that those who choose to direct the killing of others—you call it war, must lead the battle and be the first to perish for the cause. By this law, war and senseless killing are virtually eliminated in the broader universe. The old must never send the young to perish in any cause. We learned many eons ago that greed, ego and megalomania are destructive of civilized life. If the cause is seemingly just or unavoidable, the makers of this thought must submit themselves to the battle and be the first to draw and taste blood . . . their own or that of their enemy. It is the law of the peaceful universe."

"Do I understand that you, the Zeta, are willing to save the Humans of Earth from the Greys and destroy yourselves in the process?" Ed asked.

"You understand correctly."

"And you ask only that we as Humans open the door to a peaceful integration of your race with that of the Human?"

"You understand correctly. Let me clarify our understanding." The Zeta continued, "America presents the best opportunity for this to happen. Your planet is hospitable to us. Your history is that of welcoming the immigrant, the one who is different, even alien if you prefer. Your nation is the leader of the free world, the leader in innovation and expansion. We want to be a part of this and share with you the many elements of progress we possess. We tried to trade with the supposed leaders of America to achieve this end.

"We shared concepts of energy and advanced medical skills on the promise of acceptance. We were denied the fruits of this promise because of their treachery and deceit. They would not allow us to have contact with Humans. We were treated as subjects of study and investigation. Those who claimed to be from your government deceived and humiliated us. Will you be different from them?"

Sarpanit stood, her head held high and steady. "Will you accept our word, the word of the Nefilim, that this travesty will not be repeated in our alliance? Even though it may take several Human generations to make the acceptance complete, we will continually work toward it"

The Zeta also stood and gave a bow of courtesy to Sarpanit. Only one spoke and the other nodded his agreement. "We accept the word of the Nefilim without question. Although you are far younger in the Universe than we are, we have noted with extreme pleasure the progress you have made. We look forward to the same progress being made by the Humans on their planet. We know you will continually help them as we seek to do in their time of need. We acknowledge that full acceptance of our race will require understanding and preparation among the many types of their race. We will assist you in this preparation."

The Zeta looked directly at Chris and Nancy, "Will you Humans make the same assurance?"

Chris and Nancy stood with Sarpanit. Nancy indicated that Chris could speak for both. Chris said simply, "We are overcome with many feelings, but answer with clarity and honesty; we join with you in this effort to save humanity, and will lead our people to the best of our ability to grant you the acceptance you have sought and will earn. Our generations are short but we will begin the process that will make acceptance of your race on Earth as you wish."

Sarpanit said, "Let it be so. How do we begin?"

The Zeta gestured toward the opposite end of the table with the Grey sitting there with his head down. "Our brother Grey has heard our pact and will report to the others. He knows that we know where they hide and can track their movements. He knows that we will begin immediately to keep our pledge to the Nefilim and the Human. He will report that the Galactic Federation approves our intervention into the affairs of Earth in this instance and will support our efforts to eliminate the malevolent intentions and actions of the Greys. He knows that many Zetas will perish . . . but all of the Greys will cease to exist." The Zeta turned again to Sarpanit, "We have begun; the Grey may leave the meeting now!"

The Grey immediately left the room with the Zetas close behind. Sarpanit, Ed and Anna along with the McIvers remained in thoughtful silence. Sarpanit broke the spell, "I hope your first contact with aliens other than us wasn't too disturbing."

"I soon forgot they were aliens," Chris answered. "When discussing a common cause . . . like survival, differences are soon noticed less. Anyway, you look like us . . . or we look like you . . . or!

Ed's booming laugh filled the room. "Point made, Chris."

Sarpanit looked at Chris and Nancy with a serene smile. "Before the Nefilim were created, our legends and oral tradition tells us there was a Creative Force that sensed a place in the galaxy for a race like us . . . and we were created for the same purpose, to serve this Creative Force. Over time, we evolved into many different colorations and shapes, depending on where we lived on the planet Nibiru. This Creative Force adjusted our DNA many times to give us even greater abilities to fulfill our destiny. This intervention into our development eventually led us to our present state of enlightenment and capability.

"When we, the Nefilim, created the first Humans to serve us, we were on the path of realizing that even those of us who looked and acted different were of our race. During the nearly half million years since our ancestors came to Earth and created Humans, we have brought our race together and welcomed other races onto our planet, the Zetas being one of them. We have developed a close bond. It's important to know that the Zetas existed long before there were Nefilim. They helped us bring our race together, just as they will help bring Humans together.

Sarpanit sat down again and continued, "They know this will not be an immediate thing; that it will take generations of Human change and development. They are patient and understanding, but they want us to begin as soon as possible to prepare for their acceptance. The ultimate goal of the Nefilim is for the Human race to be accepted into the Galactic Federation. The Nefilim are assisting; the Zetas are assisting and the plan is in place for us to begin. I'm certain they will begin their part of the bargain immediately."

*   *   *

The International Web was totally taken by reports of abduction and murder of Humans by the Greys. Fear stalked every part of the Earth, and as instructed, people gathered in large groups, hoping to escape the notice of the Greys or present too many for the Greys to handle without interference. This grouping became even stronger when reports reached the Web of the Greys coming down to grab individuals strayed from a group and being repulsed by attacking Humans who saw the beams of light and were courageous enough to rush toward them. Nevertheless, the peace had been shattered by the Greys and once again, Earth was subject to ruthless invaders.

Within hours of the meeting on the Mother Ship, a complete replay of the conversation and results were on the Web. Humans gathered in amazement, looking at the single Grey who looked rather puny and the stately Zetas who promised to fight off the invading Greys. Crowds would stand and cheer when the Zetas appeared on the screen. They were equally awed by the beautiful Sarpanit, Ed and his wife Anna and their Human representatives, Chris and Nancy. This was played over and over until every Human on Earth had a chance to see it.

* * *

South of Los Angeles, three individuals were settling in for the night when the bright lights appeared and blinded them. They knew it was the Greys and they began to loose control of their bodies when the lights suddenly went off and were replaced by a soothing iridescent glow. The three Humans ran together out of fear when they saw the five small Greys looking about them in confusion, their large heads bobbing, their arms flailing in protective movements.

They were the first to report that one being they recognized as a Zeta, because of size and garment, actually gathered the Greys into his arms . . . and they all simply evaporated. They simply disappeared, all of them! As if by magic, the reports of abductions ceased to appear on the Web as more and more reports of the Greys' being evaporated by the Zetas appeared. Within hours, the Web was silent about any more abductions and deaths.

*   *   *

It was Ed who appeared on the screen at first light of day in America. He stood alone in a field of flowing wheat; his backdrop was the low governmental complex in Kansas. The sky was a brilliant blue with small wisps of clouds indicating a beautifully clear day. He smiled and began:

"The problem with the Greys is over; they are no longer close to Earth." After a pause he continued with a more somber tone, "We know many of you have lost loved ones during this rampage of the Greys. From the Nefilim, we Hybrids and all the Humans involved, we express our heart felt sympathy for your grief. We also express our appreciation to the Zetas for making the terror go away. As you heard in the broadcast of the meeting aboard the mother ship, the Zetas promised to dispose of the Greys and did so at their own peril. Many Zetas were lost in ridding us of the Greys. We are deeply indebted to them and will know much more about them in the future.

Meanwhile, what remained of the Greys, fully understanding the Zetas would hunt them out and destroy all of them, have left Earth for good. The Zetas will remain close to Earth and will, from time to time make additional contact with Humans. It will not be unusual to see their ships in our skies. Now, when one sees a UFO or unusual space ship, you can be certain it is the Zetas and they are our friends. They will be sharing much in the way of technology and medical procedures with Humans. We will benefit greatly from their involvement with the people of Earth.

Meanwhile, go about your lives and have no fear. Continue rebuilding and creating. We will keep you informed of any and all changes and opportunities that present themselves. Let us know how you are doing! Perhaps we can be of some assistance. The time has come when we say, 'Your government is here to help you,' *we mean it!* Live in peace and seek happiness. I'll talk with you later. I'm Ed Berkowicz."

CHAPTER
15

The governmental complex in Kansas was on full alert this day. There had been plenty of notice that the subject at hand was perhaps the most pressing in a recovering America. At the appointed time, the amphitheatre type room for public hearings was full to the rafters with standing room taken. A delegation of six women and one man had been selected from quite a few who wanted to be a part of this day. There was a different electricity in the air; far different from the contentious hearings of the past when political differences framed every question. This was a day of hope with the excitement of a completely different way of doing business. Open honesty prevailed as the meeting was opened.

"Madam Chairman, I bring a proposal from the majority of our child bearing age women in this district. We have been in touch with many other districts in America and it's been decided among us that ours would be the first to be presented as a model for the other groups ready to present themselves. In short, we believe that under the proper circumstances and with reasonable conditions, we are ready to fulfill our responsibilities to populate the Human race. We have fully discussed this with our partners and with the conditions proposed accepted, they are ready to be fathers to their own children."

The Chairman responded, "We were of course advised of this and are more than willing to hear all of the conditions you advocate. All twelve of us are open to the discussion and are ready to hear you. We have all the audio and video equipment in place so that anyone who chooses may audit these proceedings. Are you ready to begin?"

"We are, and thank you."

A very attractive woman of about thirty years approached the microphone, sat down and looked into the camera as practiced. She smiled, a little nervously, and laid out her notes on the table.

"My name is Jennifer Cook. I'm 31 years old and have been married to Kenneth for five years. We planned to have children the very year the Nefilim came and we were quite angry when it was known there would be no Human births . . . indefinitely. We now see the wisdom of this decision. We have dedicated ourselves to raising three children who came to us during that first year, two from Kenneth's sister who passed away and a third from unknown parents. We love these children like our own and they are a wonderful part of us. We will continue to love and cherish these children if granted the right to create our own child." Four more women came to testify . . . and one man. None spoke for more than three minutes but all presented a picture of young America being ready to repopulate. When all had finished, one of the Hybrid/ Human women on the council asked a relevant question of great and general interest . . . but quite different in this new world of life on planet Earth.

"We know you are all aware of the influx of the Indigo Children starting some time ago. Their time is indeed now as they grow into maturity and help move us along into a new world. Have you considered the great possibility of other reincarnated souls being your first children? Are you aware of the many 'other than Earth' entities wanting to come to this planet and be part of the Human experience?"

The petitioning group looked at each other in agreement and the first young woman to speak, Jennifer, answered for them.

"Yes, we are very much aware . . . and prepared to accept it. During these past years much has been learned about genetics and the influx of other races. We are given to understand by the Nefilim that such births would be not only natural but in keeping with where the Human destiny lies. We will all be stronger because these good souls choose to be born on Earth. We are assured that those born to us will first learn from us . . . then teach us. Even though we are assured the children would be fully Human and not look or act like unwanted aliens, and would bear resemblance to parents, some women are afraid to birth these reincarnating life forces. They will forgo the experience of childbirth until they learn more about the possibilities. Ken and I are willing to accept the experience."

"What other conditions do you propose?" A council member asked.

Another woman approached the table and indicated she would address the conditions they felt were reasonable.

"Madam Chairman and council members, the proposed conditions are quite simple. In that deception and deceit are generally no longer a problem when a marriage union is agreed upon, we feel that any specific restrictions or conditions imposed by any form of deciding authority would only invite dissension and division among us. Assuming fertility is restored to the Human race, could it be restored only in regions of the planet where adequate progress in civility and nonviolence have been established, and withheld where progress is slower?"

"We had anticipated this question and can answer yes, that can be accomplished."

"Thank you. Now that we are free of religious rules and other equally onerous backward social pressures, can our government involve itself in an extensive informational campaign to explain Human sexuality to the entire population, and fully support education of our youth to the realities of premature or irresponsible sexual activity?"

"Yes!"

"Thank you. With the understanding that the pleasure of sexual relations will continue to occur among Earth's people, can the government assure women of the availability of birth control measures if desired?"

"Yes."

"Thank you. In the event of an unwanted or unexpected pregnancy, can the government assure that the woman may chemically terminate such a pregnancy in a timely manner and without unjust recrimination?"

"Yes."

"Thank you. With the understanding that matters of disease, addiction and severe deformity be left to local communities and their councils, can the government see that profit from the buying and selling of babies, usually disguised as 'adoption rules' be eliminated?"

"Yes, we can!"

"Thank you, Madam Chairman. That is the extent of our concerns and conditions that we feel can be granted and controlled by an enlightened and benevolent government. We recognize that it is impossible to legislate morality and even more impossible to eliminate Human errors and poor decisions. We ask only for America to be reinstated in Human fertility under the conditions we have asked of you and with these conditions, be able to repopulate our Nation. Allow us to demonstrate our maturity as we proceed into the new world ahead of us."

*   *   *

"Will they do it?" Jeannie Neal asked of her husband Don after turning off the screen.

"Hell yes, they will! You've heard Ed talk about this day coming many times in the past year. This is the only thing that stands between the American people and the Nefilim . . . and they are both ready to get rid of it."

"Why did it have to happen in the first place, Don?"

"Because of starving, diseased and addicted mothers giving birth to starving, diseased and addicted kids all over the planet, the USA being no exception. Because of Human males taking their pleasure anywhere they could and making babies no one could take care of, the USA being no exception. And because of mothers getting pregnant as soon as they were healed up from popping out the last one, because their religion demanded it . . . the USA being no exception."

"Sounds pretty stupid when you put it that way." Jeannie responded.

"What sounds even more stupid is the way American politics bought into the abortion debate. Be it right or wrong, abortion was the law of the land . . . and nobody really wanted to get rid of it. The vast majority of the nation was for 'woman's rights,' but would anybody step up and say so? Hell no! They had bought into the Roman Catholic drama, hook, line, and sinker. The pope had lots of votes everybody wanted. No one wanted to offend the Catholics. Hence, constipation of politics and lots of religious posturing. Thank god, that's gone!"

"Didn't the pope at one time threaten to excommunicate any American legislator who supported 'choice?'" Jeannie kind of wrinkled her nose when asking.

"Yep! That didn't get talked about much, did it? But it happened! The story died from the precious press, but it was just like the judge saying, 'the jury will disregard that testimony.' The deed was done and the church knew it. They didn't have to pursue the subject and some of our cowardly politicos simply rolled over. Not only did the church have the votes . . . it had the dollars, too."

"Will there ever be anything like the Roman church again?" Jeannie asked.

"No, I don't believe there will be. Their age is over. It's interesting that the big lie lasted so long in the first place. They destroyed knowledge and replaced it with their own truths. We never recovered completely. A friend of mine once wrote, *'The Roman Catholic church was the worst thing that ever happened to the western world'* I'm afraid he was right. Their attitude about women, starting with Paul's admonition about "women being silent," and the intentional lies about Mary Magdalene afflict Catholic women to this day. Their protection of child molesting priests should have undone them, but it didn't! Finally, knowledge and truth have destroyed them.

*   *   *

America began to prepare for a baby boom that would exceed anything dreamed about following WWII. Names were being bandied about for this new generation that received a 91% approval from a voting population of 98%. It was the first national referendum vote taken by the government in Kansas and it was the first generation of automatic information gathering anybody had seen. Names were being chosen, the watch for the first baby born was started and a nation celebrated. Businesses catering to babies began to take form—again!

Another very positive change was at hand. Child rearing with love and discipline was being talked about everywhere. The day of making the child a spoiled and uncontrollable individual was over. They were to be cared for and loved, but not allowed free rein of their immature and instinctive self centered actions. A firm position was taken that there would be no child pornography or any form of child exploitation tolerated . . . at all! The violent video games were gone as well. Anything that promoted and/or glorified violence, wanton destruction or demeaned any person was not tolerated.

*   *   *

Ed, Anna, Chris and Nancy had their hands full with the various delegations that arrived in Kansas for the very short but highly productive debate on the refertilization of America. With a positive outcome, various delegations from all over the globe wanted to be heard, and they were allotted a time. There was some resentment on the part of many areas of the world, that America was the seat of this discussion. Many nations were reminded of the gallant effort of America to host and maintain a United Nations and their often inconsistent and obstructionist actions. They were told in no uncertain terms they were not yet ready for this step but would be helped along as they were willing to change . . . and become a part of the change in Humanity.

The Middle East and some parts of the Far East still resisted any change from their poisoned positions of senseless hate and blind religious fanaticism. They were told that a continued path of self-destruction could lead to their *extinction* if not corrected in time.

Some tried to resort to violent demonstrations and civil wars between rival sects. This was quickly smothered by removing religious and other leaders who would not face the realities of the time. Many persons were so damaged by their lifetimes of hating that they were permanently removed.

Eventually, things calmed down and some semblance of order was restored in Kansas. The central location of government proved advantageous. The less cumbersome form of government allowed more to get done and the absence of deception and deceit ruled out the advantage-seeking special interests and lobbies. In truth, the old adage that 'all politics is local' prevailed and the central government was not the seat of power and money that corrupted the failed Republic of America. The co-operative autonomy of the various areas of the land was working wonderfully. It was a working reenactment of the original concept of the United States. This time around, openness, candor and 'what's good for the nation' replaced the old politics as usual.

*　　*　　*

"What happened to the tired old debates about homosexuality and same-sex marriage?" Chris asked in an after-dinner session. The mood was relaxed.

Chris, Ed, Anna and Nancy were sitting on a small deck facing the evening sunset at the end of a busy day. Helping along with the reforming and ever developing government center was a greater chore than ever imagined, but they were gaining!

"I'd say that pious, self-righteous defenders of various religious morality persuasions have found better things to do." Ed said quietly "I hope we've learned that in many things, there is no right or wrong or good and bad! Some things simply are!"

"There are qualifications, though, Anna said. If 'whatever is' is destructive, evil and demeaning or damaging to the community as a whole, then it needs to be addressed. But judging anybody by interpreted and convoluted rules of a religious belief is inherently destructive."

"I've seen some pretty bad things happen in the military where gays were concerned. Many good people were drummed out of the service because of their stated preference. I'm sure you saw that too, Ed," Chris offered.

"I saw worse from the heterosexuals! When females became a big part of the military, pregnancy stripped too many good people from the ranks, but that was to be expected . . . and almost accepted as part of throwing healthy young men and women together.

Here again was the great wisdom of badly flawed reasoning and pressure from special interest groups."

Ed sat quietly for a while, and then began to speak as the statesman he had become.

"I think the bottom line is that government needs to keep its nose out of other people's affairs, literally! We allowed too many issues to become national political debates, many times to cover up or pass over the more important issues that would call for courage to address. I'm afraid the national leadership of the past didn't really possess that courage. Incumbency and acrimony made too many of the too long leaders fat and ineffective. Far too many of the social debates were framed and fanned by the wrong people.

"It's my fondest hope that never again will we see such divisions as liberal or conservative, secular and non-secular or republican or democrat. Their polarization and endless warfare tore this nation apart. We've always had just three great powers in this nation. They were government, corporations and religion. Their struggle for domination of the common man became even more complicated when two of the three would form a convenient union to grab for control. Of course the corporations eventually held sway when their motives were simply defined as: grow big, grow strong, and grow rich.

"The corporations accomplished this by doing a very simple thing. The greatest conflict of interest America faced and could never address was the function of *lawyers making laws*. The corporations educated and hired lawyers, supported their political election campaigns and watched them rise to positions of power in policy making. America, once declared a nation of laws, became a nation of lawyers. That way, the corporations became government and the lawyers in government became supporters of corporations.

"What became of the third leg, religion? It has always floundered over petty little matters of doctrine and sacraments. Government was very wise to encourage complete religious freedom in America. Religion has always been the one thing that could cause people to rise up and overthrow oppression . . . or be the oppressor if it was united! By assuring freedom to all religions and even sects, it guaranteed there would be no unity." Ed continued to speak in his deep, melodious voice.

"I feel true sorrow for the many who bet their entire lives on the promises religion made, and now find it all to be a hollow shell. Long ago, when the Apostle Paul created a new religion out of many that had come before and it was eventually declared the law of the land, we had been encouraged and even forced to accept man-made ideas about life and death. Nothing much had changed up until three years ago. Much of mankind had been assured that Faith and Belief was all they needed to achieve immortality, and an omnipotent God would certainly micro-manage their everyday life. I see many struggling with this rather incomprehensible belief today. It's another condition that will be erased only by time and new generations of the enlightened."

*   *   *

Within the next few months, the role of the pure Nefilim on earth had diminished to the extent that Sarpanit met with Ed several times to further expand his role in Earth leadership. There was no big meeting or announcement, but it became common knowledge that Edwin T. Berkowicz was the official ambassador from the Nefilim to America. The awakening of many Humans with Nefilim heritage had provided an untold depth of leadership to the land. Their influence and the enlightened Humans were to be found in every part of the nation's workings.

Don and Jeannie Neal had found their home again in the Indianapolis area and were a large part of the educational efforts of America. Don wasn't writing so much now as lecturing and mentoring. He and Jeannie often traveled to many parts of the globe to meet with progressive movements to bring reluctant fringe peoples into the fold of understanding the new world. Don had never attempted a novel, but was now working on one with the able assistance of Jeannie, who still edited his work for him.

Surprisingly, Chris and Nancy had taken up residence in Washington DC, which was now one big historical district. Nancy had accepted the position as Curator of the Smithsonian Institute and Chris was deeply involved with his continued learning in the fields of Archeology and Anthropology. Both were in their respective Shangri-Las and loved every minute with the visitors to the *American Museum of History*.

*   *   *

In due time, Ed and his able wife Anna said to a delegation of Zetas, "Yes, the facility at the fabled Area 51 in Nevada is ready to receive your Earth Mission. All of these previously super-secret government testing grounds have been set aside for your use. We understand there are some components there, particularly at Groom Lake, that could be especially helpful for your adjustments to Earth's gravity and atmosphere. The select group of Nefilim, Humans and Hybrid Humans will be on hand to welcome you. Everybody has been told to expect the lights from your ship upon arrival. You might want to do a 'parade lap' around the area to show off your beautiful craft. Welcome to planet Earth, our friends." Showing his now famous smile, Ed said, "With your help, we will work hard to be invited to join the Galactic Federation. May we all live long and prosper in our relationship."

Finis

ABOUT THE AUTHOR

Cliff Bush was born, raised and educated in the Hoosier state. A quiet and thoughtful man in his mid-seventies, his passions are history, religion and what's next. With a background in the ministry, broadcasting and political writing, Cliff enjoys telling people about what he's learned from pioneers like Von Daniken, Sitchin and others who dare to explore the past and question the present. He and his wife of many years, Karen, own a business in Indianapolis; enjoy family, friends, boating and social activities.

To order books
by Clifton H. Bush

please contact

BOOKMASTERS
(800) 537-6727